Disaster Bay

Ann Evans

Hippo

For Christopher and Rachel

Scholastic Children's Books
Commonwealth House, 1–19 New Oxford Street,
London WC1A 1NU, UK
a division of Scholastic Ltd
London ~ New York ~ Toronto ~ Sydney ~ Auckland

First published by Scholastic Ltd, 1997

Text copyright © Ann Evans, 1997

ISBN 0 590 19249 3

All rights reserved
Typeset by TW Typesetting, Midsomer Norton, Avon
Printed by Cox & Wyman Ltd, Reading, Berks.

10 9 8 7 6 5 4 3 2 1

Chapter 1

"It's a complete waste of money," Amber Marsden shouted over the jangle of noise.

Her cousin cast her one of his infuriating grins and continued weaving his way through the crowded games arcade.

The flashing lights from the fruit machines and space invaders made Amber blink. Her eyes hadn't quite got used to the darkness of the arcade after the brilliant sunshine outside.

"Dean, come on, let's get out of here. It's too stuffy."

"OK, in a second," Dean said. "Just one go on my favourite machine."

She wished she was outside now. In the fresh air where she could breathe. Away from the crowds and the buzzing, beeping, blaring jangle of noise and lights. Instead she was trailing after her cousin, growing more and more irritated now that she fully understood the reason why her aunt and uncle had invited her to spend the summer holidays with them.

She was nothing more than a glorified baby-sitter – or minder, considering Dean was the same age as her. In years if not in maturity.

He was taller too by a couple of inches, with copper-coloured hair, a face full of freckles and mischievous blue eyes.

"Your mum said I wasn't to let you spend all your money in the arcades."

Grinning, Dean rolled a ten-pence piece between finger and thumb. "Ten pee, hardly a fortune."

"But it won't stop at ten pence, will it."

He winked infuriatingly. "Trust me, I'm an expert."

Amber groaned. "You're a pain!"

He took off again, treading a well-worn path between the old pinball machines and the virtual reality racing cars. He stopped at a long glass machine with shelves that moved to and fro, brimming with ten-pence pieces. Dean studied which of the shelves looked the most ready to give up its fortune to him.

"One go," Amber reminded him, narrowing her deep blue eyes.

"That's all I'll need."

She pushed her long straight blonde hair back from her face and glanced around at the other people playing the machines. It seemed such a waste of money. She watched a tall, thin girl of about her own age, feeding coin after coin into a greedy fruit machine, not bothered that she wasn't winning. She simply stood there, a glazed expression on her face, pouring money into the slot as if she had an endless supply.

"Look at her," Amber whispered to her cousin. "She's put pounds and pounds into that machine."

"Perhaps she's rich."

"Or stupid."

Dean winked. "Watch the expert."

"What are you up to?"

With a furtive glance over his shoulder he sent his ten pence rolling down the chute.

But just before the coin rattled on to the shelf, Dean stooped, put his shoulder to the machine and gave it an almighty shove.

An avalanche of money clattered into the trays.

"Don't!" Amber hissed. "You'll get us thrown out!"

Without a care in the world, Dean casually gathered his winnings and strolled towards the exit.

Amber ran after him. "That's cheating. You'll get into trouble."

His blue eyes sparkled with devilment as the July sunlight blazed down to greet them. "Only if they catch me."

"No wonder your parents asked me to keep an eye on you!"

He headed jauntily towards a drinks kiosk. "I only spent ten pee, didn't I? Want a Coke?"

"I'll buy my own, thanks," replied Amber, digging deep into the back pocket of her shorts, and dreading the thought of the next six weeks.

Hayborough-on-Sea was a lovely old sea-side town, there was some beautiful countryside and views that she longed to sketch ... only she doubted she'd get a minute to herself with Dean to watch from dawn to dusk.

They bought a can of drink each and wandered lazily along the promenade. At the height of the summer season it was bustling with holidaymakers enjoying the seaside attractions – miniature motor racing, go-karts, trampolines, crazy golf.

"I quite fancy going on the beach," Amber remarked hopefully. That sea looked glorious.

"OK, but not here."

"Why? What's wrong with here?"

"This is where the holidaymakers hang out."

"*I'm* a holidaymaker..." She stopped. She was talking to herself. Dean was hanging around by the crazy golf. A man and woman and their little boy were playing.

Amber sat down on a bench and waited, assuming Dean knew them. Eventually he caught her up.

"There's a secret cove I know," he said, tossing a golf ball into the air and catching it. "We'll go there if you like."

Amber's eyes blazed. "You've stolen one of

their golf balls!" At the same instant the toddler let out a mournful wail.

"They'll get him another," Dean said dismissively, dropping the ball on to the concrete and dribbling it along with his feet.

"Take it back!" Amber shouted.

"It's only a golf ball."

"Take it back! Now!"

"OK, OK, no need to get stressed."

He sauntered back to the crazy golf and pretended to pick the ball up from just out-side the arena. "Hey! Is this what he's crying about ... there you go, little fella."

Shrugging off the grateful thanks of the parents, Dean jogged back to where Amber stood glaring furiously.

"What's up?" he asked, wide-eyed and innocent.

With a despairing groan, Amber shook her head and walked on.

She had a distinct feeling that the next six weeks were going to be anything but boring with Dean around!

Chapter 2

"So where's this secret cove then?" asked Amber.

His eyebrows wiggled. "Walk this way…"

They headed along the coastal pathway, leaving the noise and chaos of the fairground and shops behind them, to where the only sound was the waves dragging the pebbles over the beach. It made a soft shushing, singing sound, broken only by the occasional harsh cries of gulls gliding and dipping overhead.

Amber breathed deeply, and brushed her long straight blonde hair from her eyes. "Just smell this air, Dean, it's so fresh. And these cliffs are magnificent. Oh and that ocean way down there... I love places like this, don't you? So peaceful, not a soul for miles."

"You like it here then?" he mused, sauntering along, hands stuffed into the pockets of his baggy shorts.

"It's perfect," she sighed.

"I'd better not spoil it for you then."

The brief feeling of euphoria was shattered. "Meaning?"

He pulled a face. "Oh, nothing."

"Dean Brewster, what are you getting at?"

"Nothing. You like it here, so I'm not going to spoil it by telling you."

She felt like throttling him. "Telling me what?"

"That it's haunted," he muttered in a quiet voice, and turned away to stare out to sea.

Amber burst out laughing. "Oh, ghosts, is that all!"

"You aren't scared of ghosts and things then, that's good."

"Well of course I'm not, because there's no such thing."

"Good. I'm glad you think so."

"I do."

"OK, fine," said Dean, glancing uneasily over his shoulder.

Amber grinned. "It won't work, you know."

"What?"

"You! You're trying to scare me. Well I don't scare that easily. I don't believe in spooks or ghouls or spectres…"

"Nor phantoms on horseback?"

A cold shiver ran suddenly, unexpectedly, down her spine, and her confidence faltered for a second. Then she laughed and said, "No, definitely not phantoms on horseback. Honestly Dean, what a load of old rubbish."

They walked on, across the headland until they came to a section of cliff that had slipped away at some time, leaving a stepping-stone stairway down to the beach.

"This is the cove I was telling you about," said Dean. "It's called Slipper Bay, because the cliff here is made of black slipper clay. Every time there's a storm another bit of cliff slips away. It's going to be quite a sight when the house goes over. Hope I'm around to see it. It's going to be pretty spectacular!"

"What house?"

"The house where the phantom used to live about two hundred years ago – before he became a phantom of course." He pointed ahead, to a huge mansion-type house in the distance, teetering on the brink of the cliff.

Amber gasped. "That looks lethal! No one lives there now, do they?"

"Not any more. Not since Lord Devlin, the phantom, plunged to his death over these cliffs."

"And his ghost still haunts them," she said, trying to laugh the whole thing off. But strangely it didn't seem quite so unbelievable now she could see the house where this phantom, this Lord Devlin, once lived.

And these cliffs where he died...

"Come on," Dean yelled, clambering down the rocky slope to the beach. "And watch out for the moss on the rocks, it's slippery."

The afternoon sun was at its highest as she began to pick her way down the boulders. But something made her glance back, to the cliff top. She was at eye-level to the lush grass, and the hot afternoon sun created a shimmering heat haze over the ground, distorting

10

everything.

Far off in the distance she thought she glimpsed someone. A rider – or riders, on horseback, capes billowing. But in the shimmering heat haze, it could have been a mirage – a trick of the light.

Amber rubbed her eyes and looked again.

There was nothing there. She had imagined it.

But despite the heat of the day, she shivered.

Chapter 3

"You're very quiet tonight, Amber dear," Aunt Joan remarked as she cleared away the dinner dishes.

Amber tried to shake the strange unsettling feeling that had remained with her all afternoon. She didn't believe in ghosts, never had, never would. What she'd seen had been a trick of the light. Either that or a real ordinary human horse-rider – or riders.

Only who wore capes these days? And how could they have been there one second and gone the next?

"She's tired I bet," Uncle Dave remarked, taking his coffee over to the plump armchair in front of the television. He stretched out his long legs and wiggled his toes. "This sea air takes some getting used to."

Amber collected up the dessert bowls and followed her aunt through to the kitchen. "I am a bit tired, we went to Slipper Bay today. Dean says it's supposed to be haunted by a phantom or something..." She made light of it, expecting her aunt to dismiss it as a lot of nonsense.

"So they say," said Aunt Joan, startling Amber. "We've got a book that tells the whole story somewhere. Dean! Have a look for that book – *Local Legends*."

"I'm using it," a wailed reply drifted back from the other room.

"He's reading?" Aunt Joan gasped in disbelief. "My Dean – reading? I knew you'd be a good influence on him, Amber."

Amber smiled feebly. She doubted that anyone would be a good influence on Dean.

"You know, Amber," Aunt Joan said quietly, "the school holidays would have been a nightmare for me if you weren't here. Heaven only knows what mischief Dean would have got up to left to his own devices, now I'm out at work all day."

"You work for a charity office, don't you Aunty Joan? Do you like it?"

"Love it! Although I did think twice about taking it on with Dean being such a handful. You'd think he'd know right from wrong, wouldn't you, with his dad being a policeman!"

Amber laughed. "That's boys for you."

With the washing-up finished, Amber and her aunt relaxed in the living room. Dean was playing on his computer, working the controls like a demon.

"I thought you said you were reading," Aunt Joan said disappointedly.

"Nope," Dean muttered, not taking his eyes from the screen.

"You certainly did, Dean!" Aunt Joan said crossly. "When I asked you to look for that book on legends. You said you were reading it."

"I didn't say I was reading it. I said I was using it."

Aunt Joan turned in exasperation to her husband – he was sound asleep, his head lolling on to his chest.

Amber understood exactly what Dean meant. She strode over to him and jabbed her finger on the pause button.

"Hey!"

"'Scuse me," she said, smiling sweetly as she lifted his monitor off a thick blue book entitled *Local Legends*. "Hold this a minute." And she deposited the monitor into his surprised arms. She retrieved the book then, still smiling, replaced the monitor on the table and pressed play.

"It's too low now," Dean complained.

"You can have it back in a while… Oh watch out, Dean, you've just been terminated!"

"What!"

Exchanging grins with her aunt, Amber settled down to read up on the legend of their local phantom.

Lying in her bed that night, Amber found the story of the tragic Lord Devlin going round and round in her head.

He had been a wealthy nobleman who had built the house on the cliffs for his new bride Isabella. The house then had been well back from the cliff edge. But slowly, year by year, more and more of the cliff had gradually eroded away.

One stormy night two hundred years ago, Lord Devlin and Isabella had quarrelled. She had run from the house into the storm. Lord Devlin had gone after her. But there was no sign. And as the mist swept in and the rain lashed down, he mounted his white stallion and rode across the cliff tops calling her name.

In the pitch-black, moonless night, he had misjudged the edge of the cliff and rode tragically over it to his death.

Isabella had returned home later that night, found her husband gone and waited for his return.

It was many months later that his body – or what was left of it – was found, tangled in fishermen's nets way out at sea.

Isabella had remained living in the house, alone, until she died six years later – some say, of a broken heart.

Amber couldn't sleep. The story was so sad – so tragic. She sat up in bed and reached for her sketch pad. Balancing it on her knees she tried to draw what she'd seen that afternoon.

A rider, or riders in capes, galloping across the cliff tops.

But in the end she gave up. Her picture was useless. She couldn't put into black and white exactly what she'd seen – or thought she'd seen.

But then, she'd never tried to draw a ghost before.

Chapter 4

After breakfast the following morning, Amber replaced the book under Dean's computer. The story had saddened her, but worse was the thought that two hundred years on, the spirit of Lord Devlin was, supposedly, still searching for his wife.

"Make yourself some breakfast, Amber dear," said her aunt, throwing keys and purse into her handbag, and snatching a hasty sip of coffee. "Oh and a big favour, if you've nothing special planned."

"What's that, Aunty Joan?"

"A lovely old couple have moved in at Hazelfield Lodge. Dean knows the place. I met them just as they were moving in last week. Jeremy and Fiona Blythe – I was distributing leaflets asking for jumble. Mrs Blythe said she'd sort me out some bits they didn't wear much any more. Wasn't that kind? Anyway, I said we'd collect." She looked hopefully at her niece. "Would you be an angel?"

"No problem," Amber said cheerfully. "We've nothing else to do."

"Wonderful! Just bring it here and I'll go through it tonight. With luck there might be one or two things we can auction. They looked awfully well-off – well they'd have to be, wouldn't they, buying Hazelfield Lodge! Anyway, I'm late, see you tonight."

Uncle Dave came downstairs a few minutes after Aunt Joan had left for work. Amber was spreading strawberry jam on her toast.

"That looks fattening," he said with a cheerful smile. In his police uniform with his hefty black shiny shoes, he looked massive. A deterrent to any villain – but a pussy cat towards his own family. And didn't Dean know it!

"Mmm, probably," Amber smiled.

"So, what's on today's agenda for you and that rogue son of mine?" he asked, spooning coffee into a cup.

"Collecting jumble from Hazelfield Lodge for Aunty Joan."

He nodded. "Ah, the new folk. Haven't met them myself. In fact I don't think anyone around here has even set eyes on them yet."

"Aunty Joan has," said Amber, tucking into her toast. "She said they were nice."

"And rich, to be able to afford that place," remarked Uncle Dave. "Fabulous house, way out on the coastal road. Close enough for a nice sea view, and not so near that there's any danger of being bothered by crumbling cliffs."

Amber licked the last sticky crumbs from her fingers. "Like Lord Devlin's house... Uncle Dave, do you believe his ghost haunts the cliff tops?"

"According to local legend it does. Can't say as I believe it myself, but we've had quite a few sightings reported over the years."

"It's such a sad story," she said softly.

"If it interests you that much, get yourself down to the town museum, there's a whole section of exhibits taken from the Devlin house."

Her eyes lit up. "Honestly?"

"Certainly. They put a preservation order on the old house, it's a listed building or some such thing. For a long time people were allowed to go and look around at its treasures and paintings. Then, when the cliffs began to really crumble and it got too dangerous, they decided to empty the old house and move all its artefacts into the museum."

"Brilliant! I'll go this afternoon!"

"I'm not sure if the old place got cleared completely before they closed it up; rumour has it there's still a few of Isabella Devlin's own paintings left in there somewhere."

"She painted?"

He grinned. "Thought that would interest you. But you can forget about what's left in the house. There's plenty of her work in the museum to see. Anyway, the house was boarded up last year. It could go over the cliff at any time."

"And the paintings destroyed too?" said Amber, saddened at the thought.

"If they exist." He ruffled her hair. "I'll see you later. Keep an eye on that son of mine, won't you?"

Amber promised that she would.

She hoped Dean liked museums!

Chapter 5

"I hate museums!" Dean grumbled, as they walked along the coastal road dotted with fabulous sun-bleached villas with their private swimming pools.

Amber shrugged. "Please yourself. But I'm going, once we get the jumble back. How much further to Hazelfield Lodge?"

"Next house along," he said, plucking a flower from a garden only to pull its petals off and scatter them on the cobbled road.

"Must you..." The sound of horses' hooves clattering on the stony road made her heart thud. They weren't far from the cliffs – the haunted cliffs – and for a second Amber held her breath, almost too afraid to turn around.

But there was no phantom on horseback. Just three people in hard hats and jodhpurs. She almost laughed aloud at her own stupidity.

"What's up with you?" Dean asked, patting the last animal as it trotted by.

"Nothing!"

"Scared of horses, are you?"

"Course not."

"You looked scared."

"Well I'm not!" she answered, growing irritated.

"I go horse-riding sometimes," said Dean, surprising her. She hadn't thought he was interested in anything worthwhile. "There's riding stables nearby. We could go sometime."

"Great," Amber said, pushing all thoughts of ghosts from her head. "I can't ride, but I'd love to learn... Ah, is this Hazelfield Lodge?"

"Yep!"

She whistled at the sight of the elegant white-pillared house, set in beautifully laid-out gardens, with ornate pools and fountains. "Are we allowed in? It looks awfully posh!"

24

"Of course, come on."

Their approach up the wide gravel drive didn't go unnoticed. The huge oak door was thrown wide and a man stepped out. Tall and wiry with a hard narrow face and small black eyes.

"This is private property!" he yelled. "Clear off!"

"Friendly bloke," Dean muttered.

"We've come to pick up some jumble for the charity office in town – Mrs Blythe promised my aunt," Amber hurriedly explained.

A woman appeared beside him. Almost as tall, almost as thin. Both were hard-faced, with sallow complexions. "So I did. I forgot to mention it to my husband. Jeremy dear, it's those black bags in the conservatory." She spoke in a voice that sounded to Amber as if it was laid on for effect. "We won't keep you a moment."

The door was closed on Amber and Dean, and they glanced at each other.

"Who's she trying to impress with that voice?" Dean muttered.

"Us, I imagine," Amber said, frowning. "You know, that's really odd…"

"What is?"

"Your aunt said they were a nice old couple … but they're horrible!"

"Perhaps she caught them in a better mood," remarked Dean as he flopped against one of the big stone pillars and lifted his freckled face to the sun. "Hey Amber, you don't really want to go to a mouldy old museum this afternoon, do you?"

She brightened. "You bet! I can't wait to see Lady Isabella's paintings and stuff. I'd love to see what's left in their old tumbledown house too, but your dad says it's too dangerous. It's such a shame though, her paintings will be lost for ever. Bet they'd be valuable too."

Dean's eyes lit up. "Valuable … how valuable?"

"I don't know. But your dad's right, it's not worth the risk with the house being so close to the cliff edge."

"Keep away from there!" snapped Fiona Blythe suddenly. Her words cut the air like a knife as she appeared behind them with a bulging black plastic sack.

Startled, Amber swung around. "Oh we will, don't worry. My uncle's already told us…"

"Make sure you listen to him then," Fiona Blythe said. She sounded panicky and her eyes shifted nervously to her husband, who had emerged with more plastic sacks. "They mustn't go there, must they, Jeremy? They mustn't go near that boarded-up old house on the cliffs."

Jeremy Blythe dropped the sacks at Amber's feet and stepped closer to her. Towering like a bent willow. Blocking out the sun, so that she felt cold.

His eyes seemed to penetrate through her. His words were flat, emotionless. "You won't go there if you've any sense."

Amber fidgeted, acutely uncomfortable beneath his staring eyes. "We're not…"

"I'm glad to hear it. It's dangerous there. People could get badly hurt if they hang around there – killed even."

An icy cold shiver ran through Amber's body and she broke free from his unpleasant stare.

Why did he make it sound like a threat?

She and Dean gathered up the sacks, anxious to be away from here. Nervously, she made garbled conversation. Trying to relieve the tension that crackled like electricity all around them.

"You won't catch us anywhere near the place. Besides there's a legend that the cliff tops are haunted anyway…"

"By a phantom horseman!" said Jeremy Blythe.

"You've heard the legend too?" said Amber.

"It's common knowledge," he said, folding his arms, still staring down on her with cold unfriendly eyes. "You wouldn't want to bump into *him* on a dark night, would you?"

Another threat.

But she tilted her chin defiantly. She didn't like being threatened. "Actually, I don't believe in ghosts … I think it's all a load of old rubbish!"

His cold eyes narrowed. "But can you be certain? Can you take that risk?"

Her courage was deserting her. There was something evil about this Jeremy Blythe, something that made her skin prickle.

And to think her aunt said they were a lovely old couple!

She turned to her cousin. "Ready, Dean?"

"Thanks for the jumble," said Dean, but as they turned to go they walked straight into another cold, unfriendly face.

But this one was younger and vaguely familiar.

Of course – the girl in the arcade yesterday. The one with money to burn. Judging by the similarity in appearance – tall and willowy with a mean expression on her face – she was Jeremy and Fiona Blythe's daughter.

And obviously she *did* have money to burn.

But for all their wealth, it didn't seem to have made them very happy.

"Grim or what!" Dean exploded once out on the coastal road again.

Amber felt uncomfortable. She could still feel those nasty threatening eyes boring into her. They left a cold haunting sensation inside of her that she couldn't shift.

"Why did they get so uptight about us going to the old house?" she asked Dean as they hauled the sacks back towards home.

Dean shrugged. "Beats me how they even know about the place, seeing as they've only recently moved in."

"They could have gone for a walk and discovered it. It's not far from here is it?"

"Just along the coast a bit," he replied, taking his baseball cap off to wipe the sweat from his eyes. "Phew, this weighs a ton. I hope it's not all junk!"

Amber pulled a face. "Me too… You know, the way they warned us not to hang about there, I got the feeling it wasn't because they were worried about our safety."

"So what were they panicking about?"

A niggling feeling disturbed her. "I don't know, maybe they've got something to hide there."

"Who knows? Perhaps they're after the last few of Lady Isabella's paintings – or perhaps they've already nicked them, and don't want anyone finding out."

"But they're rich anyway."

"Ah, but how did they get so rich?"

"I've no idea," murmured Amber, frowning. "But the biggest mystery to me is how your mum could possibly describe them as a lovely old couple – they were absolutely horrible!"

Dean shrugged. "That's Mum for you, she sees good in everyone."

Amber shook her head. There was only one thing she saw in Jeremy Blythe, and it wasn't good...

It was evil!

Chapter 6

They eventually reached home and dumped the sacks in the kitchen. Then they made cold drinks and a sandwich, and set off out again.

Dean showed Amber where the town museum was, and waved her goodbye. "See you later."

"Aren't you coming in?"

He wrinkled his nose. "Nah, got some mates to see. Meet you back home."

Amber chewed on her lip, wondering whether he could be trusted not to get into trouble. Then again, could she trust him to wander around a museum without causing mayhem!

Deciding it was far more sensible to keep

Dean and precious antiques as far apart as possible, she walked into the cool of the museum and went eagerly in search of the Devlin collection.

It was more fascinating than she had hoped.

Isabella's jewellery was on display – and fabulous dresses in silks and velvet. And some of Lord Devlin's velvet riding capes and long boots. Poetry that Isabella had written – sad poems that told of the tremendous love she and Lord Devlin had shared. But best of all were the oil paintings – landscapes and seascapes painted by Isabella herself.

Amber wandered dreamily amongst all the exhibits, lost in thought. There were only a few other visitors to the museum, two elderly ladies whose whispered comments echoed around the cool exhibition hall. And a group of noisy lads who were keeping the museum attendant busy, as he made sure they didn't touch anything.

Amber wondered if they were friends of Dean.

"This is one of our best attractions," the attendant remarked when the lads eventually went through to the next hall, where another attendant was on duty, leaving him to straighten the rope barriers.

"It's fascinating," Amber agreed.

"Course it also attracts undesirables, the troublemakers," he complained, nodding to where the sound of the boys' laughter was coming from.

She was glad she hadn't brought Dean!

He sniffed. "You've got to have eyes in the back of your head with this job. Some people would pinch anything."

She nodded.

"I've had fossils nicked, a helmet from Roman times, a three-foot sword – beats me how they sneak 'em out, period costume gone missing, the lot."

"That's awful," Amber agreed, wishing he would leave her in peace.

"Eyes in the back… Oh not again…"

The group of boys charged back, skidding on the polished floor. The attendant gave chase, leaving her to look at the paintings and poetry in peace.

She wandered home much later, in a daze.

*　*　*

Aunt Joan sat on the living-room floor surrounded by clothing.

She looked up, grinning from ear to ear. "This is wonderful stuff. The quality is out of this world!"

Amber's eyebrows arched in surprise. The clothing did look excellent. Not the usual things people throw out as jumble. It was hard to think that the Blythes could be so generous.

Aunt Joan held a coat against her. "Pure wool. What a pity the style's for someone much older."

"Fiona Blythe isn't that old," Amber remarked, sitting down amongst the clothes and checking that nothing had been left in the pockets.

"She's no spring chicken," laughed Aunt Joan. "Anyway, I'm sure there's lots of old dears who'll pay a good price for this sort of quality. I just wish she was my size."

"Couldn't you just take the hems up?" Amber suggested.

Her aunt stared at her. "Take them up?

Don't you mean let them down?"

"No, Fiona Blythe is much taller than you."

Aunt Joan looked bemused. "She's not, she's a short little thing." The telephone ringing in the hall interrupted their argument. Aunt Joan jumped up. "'Scuse me."

Amber looked at the label in the coat. "Dean, this wouldn't have fitted Fiona Blythe. This is for a shortish, fattish person; she was tall and skinny."

Dean uttered a disinterested grunt as he wrestled intently with his computer joystick.

Amber examined some more of the clothing. Oddly, they were all the same size as the first coat.

All to fit a shorter, fatter, older person than Fiona Blythe. She examined the men's clothing. Likewise, there was nothing here that would fit either Jeremy or Fiona Blythe.

"It's not the Blythes' stuff," she informed Dean. "It can't be. But if they've just moved in they'd hardly have brought someone else's clothing with them, just to get rid of it at the first opportunity ... would they, Dean?"

"What... Ah, no! They got me."

Amber stared at the clothes spread all around her, puzzled.

"Aunty Joan," she said as her aunt returned. "Is this the stuff we brought back from the Blythes' today?"

"Yes, dear. Look, I'm sorry I have to nip out. Committee meeting that I completely forgot about."

Amber was still frowning. "And, Mrs Blythe told you it was stuff they didn't wear much any more."

"Actually," Aunt Joan confided, as she threw on her coat, and made a frantic search for her handbag, "I think she was just being kind. Donating something just to be helpful."

"Helpful – her?" Amber gasped in disbelief.

"She was sweet… Look, I have to go."

Amber had been checking the pockets as they talked. Her fingers closed around something then. "Aunty Joan – look what's in this pocket!"

"What is it?"

"A wallet!"

Dean whizzed round. "Brill … any money in it?"

"Actually yes," said Amber, counting out the five-pound notes. "Thirty-five pounds!"

"Great!" exclaimed Dean.

Aunt Joan raised her eyebrows at her son. "Don't get excited Dean, we aren't keeping it. You can take it back tomorrow."

"Aw, Mum!"

"No arguments – Amber, see it gets back to them. Now I must dash – bye."

The prospect of meeting up with the Blythe family again made Amber go cold. Although even they would have to be pleasant when they returned their money.

Wouldn't they?

She picked up the woollen coat again and pressed it to her face. There was a faint lingering scent of perfume and powder. A grey hair was tangled into the fabric. She plucked it out and laid it in her palm.

A feeling of utter sadness crept over her suddenly. A feeling that she couldn't shake off.

These clothes didn't belong to Jeremy and Fiona Blythe at all. So whose were they?

And even more puzzling was how could

they pretend to be a sweet, kind, generous couple to her aunt, and totally unpleasant to her and Dean.

It just didn't make sense.

And she intended to find out just what was going on.

Chapter 7

It looked as if no one was home when Amber and Dean wandered along to Hazelfield Lodge again the following day.

"Let's have another look at that wallet, Amber."

She passed it to him.

Dean peered at the wad of notes. "Considering they'd forgotten all about this money, they aren't likely to remember how much was in it." He cast her an innocent look. "Could have been thirty-five pounds ... maybe it was only twenty-five!"

"No, Dean! It's all going back, every penny."

"But they'll never know."

"That's not the point, now give me the wallet."

He held it over his head and jogged just out of Amber's reach.

"Dean, you pain!"

"Come and get it..." Something fluttered out of the wallet and landed on the ground.

Amber picked it up. It was a photograph. A photo of an elderly white-haired couple, looking suntanned and happy.

"Who are they?"

Amber shook her head, taking the opportunity of recapturing the wallet. "We'll ask, shall we?"

No one shouted at them to clear off as they walked up the drive, and no one answered the doorbell.

"Must be out," said Amber.

"Good!" grumbled Dean. "Just shove the wallet – and all that lovely money – through the letterbox and let's go."

"Suppose we'll have to... Oh! Can you smell smoke?"

Dean stepped back from the house and looked up. "Looks like a bonfire, around the back."

"Come on," she said, heading around to the

back of the house with Dean at her heels, complaining he'd got much better things to do.

Jeremy and Fiona Blythe were at the bottom of their huge garden throwing things on to a blazing bonfire. They didn't notice Amber and Dean approach. As they got near, Amber was amazed to see just what they were burning.

More clothes! Clothes that looked as good as the ones they'd given away. And piles of folders and documents. But worst of all were photograph albums.

No one burnt photograph albums!

Jeremy Blythe suddenly swung around, his narrow face twisted with surprise and then anger. "What the... Get the devil out of here, you little trespassers. I'll have the law on you. This is private property."

"I'm sorry," Amber murmured, backing off from him and the intense heat of the blaze. "We did ring your bell. We've brought something back. It was in a suit pocket."

Fiona Blythe pushed her husband aside. She looked just as agitated as him and struggled to appear relaxed. "All right Jeremy dear, I'll see to it. So, what did you find in Jeremy's old suit?"

"This," said Amber, handing her the wallet. She was puzzled that Fiona Blythe had said it was Jeremy's suit. It couldn't possibly be Jeremy's suit – it wouldn't fit!

Fiona Blythe examined the wallet.

"It's got thirty-five pounds in it," Dean said, sounding hopeful, as if there might be a reward for returning it.

"And you've brought it back – how kind." Fiona Blythe's voice stiffened. "Jeremy, perhaps we should have double-checked the jumble before letting it go."

Jeremy said nothing. He turned back to the bonfire.

"There's a photograph in there, too," said Amber. "Of an elderly couple."

Jeremy Blythe swung round. There were two spots of red darkening his sallow cheeks. He snatched the wallet off his wife and pulled out the photograph.

"Relations of yours?" Amber asked, wishing Jeremy would move so that she could get a better look at the photo albums he was burning. Why would anyone burn photographs? They were so precious.

"Parents," said Fiona Blythe.

"Yours?" asked Amber, aware that Dean was being just as nosy as her, and was trying to flick open a smouldering photograph album with his foot.

For a second Fiona and Jeremy just stared at each other, as if they didn't know the answer. And then Fiona blurted out, "His! They're his parents."

"And was it their clothes you gave us yesterday?" asked Amber, expecting to be told to mind her own business. But nevertheless she stuck with it. "We couldn't help but notice that they weren't your size."

They stared at each other again. The red spots on Jeremy's cheeks were growing darker.

"Yes, that's right," said Fiona. "How very observant of you."

"You don't like your parents much then, do you," said Dean suddenly, and everyone swung around to stare at him.

He had flicked open an album that was half in, half out of the flames.

Three or four photographs of the same elderly couple were slowly charring and curling up at the edges.

Slowly, very slowly, they were being cremated.

Chapter 8

"They're dead, OK!" snapped Jeremy Blythe, kicking the album deeper into the flames. "Now clear off, we're busy."

"Your parents are dead and you're burning their photographs!" Amber exclaimed in disbelief.

Fiona Blythe put a hand on Amber's shoulder and steered her back towards the street. Dean followed. Fiona's voice was almost sugar-coated. "My husband's parents died a short while ago. He gets upset when he's reminded of them. That's why we're disposing of all their things."

"Oh, I see," murmured Amber, glancing at Dean and seeing that he didn't believe a word of it either. "Well, we'll leave you to it then."

"I think that's best," Fiona Blythe agreed, her pinched face creasing into a sweet smile.

Amber and Dean walked in silence up the garden and out on to the coastal road.

"Did you believe a word of that?" Dean exclaimed.

"No way! No one gets rid of their parents' photographs. You might put them away in a drawer if they're too painful to look at. But you don't chuck them on a bonfire – and they lied about the suit. First she said it was her husband's, then her father-in-law's."

"What do you reckon they're up to?" Dean asked.

Amber shrugged. "Your guess is as good as mine. They're one weird family. They give me the creeps."

They had set out laden with backpacks with their swimming gear, packed lunch and Amber's art materials, ready for a lazy day on the beach. The confrontation with the Blythes had put Amber on edge though. There was something strange about that couple.

Very strange.

"Ah well, nothing much we can do," sighed Dean. "Slipper Bay?"

Amber nodded. "Suits me."

From the coastal road, they took a short cut on to the cliff path.

Within minutes they were on the warm breezy clifftop. Lord Devlin's chimney tops were just visible beyond the rolling green fields to their right.

"Where's Slipper Bay from here then, Dean?"

He climbed on to a stile and pointed left, to where the cliff path forked downwards towards the beach. "A ten-minute walk, it's not far. Anyway Amber, what were you saying about paintings left in the old house? How valuable do you reckon they are?"

She guessed what he was thinking. "Not valuable enough to get yourself killed for!"

His eyes sparkled. "Wouldn't you just love to take a peep? You're interested in art, aren't you?"

She had to admit, it was tempting. Just to take a peep in through a crack in the boarded-up window and perhaps catch a glimpse of one of the paintings before they were lost for ever – if they were still there. But she pulled a face. "It's dangerous, Dean."

"We won't go in. We can't anyway. It's boarded up."

Amber sighed. The story of Lord Devlin and Isabella intrigued her. It wouldn't hurt just to take a closer look at their old house – would it?

She made up her mind and climbed over the stile. "Go on then, only remember, we're *not* going in!"

"Course not."

They picked their way across the meadow. In one corner a herd of cows were grazing beneath the shade of some trees. A young man in wellington boots was leaning on the fence talking to the cattle.

"Hey, kids!" he called out, waving to them.

"O-Oh!" muttered Dean.

"What's wrong?"

"It's Sam, Farmer Draper's farm-hand. Pretend we haven't seen him."

"Why?"

"Because he'll probably tell us to get off his boss's land."

Amber glared at her cousin. "You mean we're trespassing! I might have known."

"Kids, over here!" Sam yelled again.

Casting Dean a withering glare, she headed towards the farm hand. "Morning," she said pleasantly.

The cows plodded away as Amber and Dean approached, only to wander up inquisitively behind them, too nervous to be stroked, however.

"And where are you two off to?" Sam asked. He had straw coloured hair and weather-beaten skin. A nice face though, Amber thought.

"Just taking a walk," said Dean.

"I hope we're not trespassing," Amber said innocently.

"Well, this is Farmer Draper's land," Sam said, glancing back at the farmhouse. A farmer with a gun under his arm and a dog at his heels was just going indoors. "He gets a bit niggled when folk leave gates open. But so long as you remember to shut gates and not scare the livestock, you're OK." His forehead crinkled like a ploughed field. "And don't mess about around the old house, that could go any day now."

"No, we won't," Dean lied.

With a wave they continued on their way across the meadow, avoiding the old house until they were sure Sam couldn't see them.

And then, keeping low, they ran down a grassy crater-like dip, where a huge chunk of the earth had sunk.

There, nestling in the crater, surrounded by rolls of barbed wire and notices warning trespassers not to enter, towered Lord Devlin's once magnificent house.

Amber stopped dead in her tracks, struck by its faded beauty. A strange, ominous feeling wrapped itself around her.

The house seemed surrounded by an aura of sadness. As if it knew its fate. Yet it stood bravely, proudly, silently waiting the awful day when wind and rain would finally loosen the earth on which it stood, and send it crashing down the cliff to its death.

Just like the master of the house, Lord Devlin – the phantom.

"I have to draw it, Dean," she whispered. "While it's still standing."

"Go on then, I'll have a look around. Doesn't look like we'll be able to get through the barbed wire anyway."

"Be careful," she warned, eagerly spreading her art materials on the grass.

She worked carefully, but with a strange sense of urgency, sketching the once proud outline of the building first. Then came the colours. The deep blue sky, the blue-grey of the stone, the hint of black paintwork that still clung to the peeling window-frames. She drew glass in the windows instead of the wooden panels that boarded them up, and left out the barbed wire.

She studied the finished work critically, wishing she was a better artist. Wishing she was as good as Isabella Devlin had been.

Dean had been exploring around the house. For the last ten minutes she hadn't set eyes on him. He reappeared just as she was closing her sketch pad and packing her things away.

He looked excited.

"Hey, Amber!"

"What?"

His face glowed.

"I've found a way in!"

Chapter 9

"Just around the back," Dean said excitedly. "Someone's cut through the barbed wire, you can just roll it out of the way. And the back door has been levered open. You just have to push it."

Amber's mouth dropped open. "You didn't go in!"

"Just popped my head in. It's pretty dark. We'll need a torch."

"I haven't got one."

"Then we'll come back tomorrow."

"Oh, I don't know Dean … it's dangerous."

"Just come and see."

Reluctantly, she followed him around to the shadowy side of the house, where moss and creeping ivy smothered the walls. Underfoot, weeds and grass sprung up from between the cracked stone slabs that had once been a pathway.

She began to feel cold.

There was a strong wind up here on the cliff – so close to the edge. The chill air brought her skin out in goosebumps and she began to shiver – or tremble.

"Dean, I don't think this is such a good idea."

"It's OK. Come on."

She trod carefully, her heart pounding. The ground here felt different. It felt unsafe – it looked unsafe. Pitted and cracked, like broken eggshells.

And all the while the wind gusted in, catching her breath, reminding her of how high up they were, and how perilously close they were to the edge.

Her head began to swim; she felt dizzy, sick. "Let's go back. It's dangerous here…"

"In a second."

There had once been a garden here, Amber realized, holding her long hair in one hand so that it didn't blow over her eyes and blind her to where she was walking. It must have been a beautiful garden two hundred years ago. There were the remains of a fountain and elegant statues and archways.

But only the remains.

The garden had been cruelly sliced in half. Half clung on to the house, crumbling and smothered in weeds, but the other half of the garden had gone. Leaving just a gaping nothingness.

Only a sheer drop to the rocks hundreds of metres below.

"We ought to go back…"

"No, wait, I'll show you," said Dean, carefully squeezing through a gap in the barbed wire fencing.

Amber's heart was thudding so painfully she could hear it beating in her ears – like drumbeats.

But she followed, avoiding the sharp barbed points. There were strands of clothing clinging to some of the wire, as if someone had caught themselves getting through.

Who? Who had broken in?

Someone inquisitive like herself maybe? Kids? Or someone curious to find the forgotten paintings. Perhaps they'd broken in to steal them. Perhaps the Blythes.

Dean pushed the back door and it creaked open. "See!"

Amber took a deep breath. They had come this far...

She peeped in. It smelt of dampness and something else. A horrible stench of something rotting.

"What's that revolting smell?" she gasped.

Dean shrugged. "Your feet?"

"Ha, ha!" she muttered, letting her eyes grow accustomed to the gloom and trying not to breathe too deeply.

This room appeared to be the kitchen. There was an old-fashioned black cooking range and a few old brass pans hanging from a beam.

No paintings that she could see. Although they would hardly be in the kitchen anyway.

She stepped back and closed the door.

"We'll need a torch if we're to see anything."

"Tomorrow then," suggested Dean and she nodded.

He dragged the barbed wire back into place, and they walked out of the shadows into the sunlight...

And into a hail of gunshot pellets.

Chapter 10

"Someone's shooting at us!"

They threw themselves flat on the ground as another loud boom exploded followed by another shower of gunshot pellets that peppered and sparked off the brick walls.

"Keep your head down!" she screamed.

"Pack it in!" he yelled with his face in the dust.

The only answer was another loud bang and the pinging of pellets on the walls above their heads.

"Why?" Amber cried. "Why is someone shooting at us?"

"I don't know," Dean wailed, his eyes wide and frightened. "What we gonna do, Amber?"

"Don't panic," she breathed, her heart pounding like a sledgehammer. "It's that farmer I bet. He had a gun didn't he, and we're on his land."

"I'm gonna report him to my dad. He can't go around shooting at people. It's against the law."

"So is trespassing!"

She felt like a sitting target there in the clearing. Further up the grassy slope were a few bushes. It was better than nothing.

"Let's make a run for that bush," Amber whispered. "We might be able to see who's firing at us from there."

"Go on then," Dean agreed, "but keep your head down."

They ran, almost on all fours, scampering like frightened rabbits. Expecting to hear the boom of the gun and the pain of gunshot hitting them at any second.

But they reached the bush in one piece and cowered there for a moment, catching their breath. Then Amber peered very cautiously through the thicket.

"See anyone?" Dean hissed.

"No … wait yes, look. There's someone just going into the trees where the cows are – see!"

Dean stood and peered over the top of the bush. "I see him! He's got a gun! See, slung over his shoulder."

"Do you recognize him?" Amber asked urgently, as he disappeared behind the trees.

Dean pulled a face. "Not really, he's too far away. I bet it was Farmer Draper. The farmhouse is just over there."

"That's the way back to *everywhere*, Dean," Amber reminded him. "The farmhouse, the coastal road, Slipper Bay, town – everywhere!"

Dean's forehead crinkled. "So it could have been anyone shooting at us."

"Not anyone," she murmured thoughtfully. "Just someone with a reason."

"I still reckon it was Farmer Draper."

She was silent for a moment as gradually her pulse slowed to something like normal speed, and the terrified tightening of her throat began to relax. "There is another possibility," she murmured.

Dean stared at her. "What?"

"The Blythes! That Jeremy was pretty odd yesterday about us not going near the old house. He could have followed us."

"Why?"

"The paintings probably. I reckon he's after them, and doesn't want anyone getting to them first."

Dean stared at her. "And he'd try and shoot us just for that?"

"Looks like it," Amber said softly, starting to tremble as the enormity of what had just happened sank in.

Possibly they'd just had a warning to keep away from here. Maybe it had been Farmer Draper scaring them off his land. Or Jeremy Blythe scaring them away from the old house.

Or possibly ... just possibly, someone had actually tried to kill them!

Chapter 11

The activities of the day were the main topic of conversation over dinner that evening.

Dean and Amber had reported the shooting to Uncle Dave down at the police station that afternoon. The police had taken the incident seriously and sent two officers out to speak to Farmer Draper.

"His gun hadn't been fired," said Uncle Dave as he tucked into his meal. "We did tests which showed it hadn't been fired in days."

Amber pushed her dinner around her plate, her appetite gone. "Maybe he's got two guns."

"He's only licensed for one."

Even Dean seemed off his food. "Maybe

he's got one gun for shooting crows and another for shooting kids."

"What were you doing up at the old house anyway?" Aunt Joan demanded. "You know how dangerous it is around there! Honestly Dave, they really ought to demolish it. It's a deathtrap."

"It's all secured, love," said Uncle Dave. "Besides, they've left it a bit late. It'd be too dangerous to send a demolition crew in now with all their heavy tackle with the place so close to the edge. Let nature take its course. It can't last much longer. Next good storm should take it, I reckon."

"But what happens if it goes over and there's people below on the beach?" Amber asked.

"That part of the beach has been fenced off ready," Dean explained. "You can't get on to the bit directly below the house."

"Barbed-wired, is it?" she murmured, thinking how easily someone had snipped through the barbed wire surrounding the house.

Her thoughts were racing. Who had done that? Was it someone anxious to get their hands on some old paintings? Or was there some other motive?

Something more sinister?

Something worth killing for?

Her thoughts returned to the Blythes. "Uncle Dave, what do you know about Mr and Mrs Blythe?"

"Not a thing, never met them. Why?"

"Because when we went round there today, they were burning a load of stuff, clothing, documents, photograph albums – photos of their parents! We thought that was really weird."

He pulled a face. "People do strange things. You certainly see that in my line of work... Any more gravy, love?"

After dinner, Amber and Dean took a walk into town. Shops remained open to cater for the holidaymakers, music drifted out from cafés and arcades and illuminations flickered on as darkness fell.

Amber enjoyed wandering around the gift shops and chose a nice ornament to take back to her mum. "Shall I get your aunt one of these Dean … Dean?"

He was nowhere to be seen, and she quickly put the ornaments down and hurried out of the shop. She spotted him talking to someone.

The Blythes' daughter.

She hung back, and waited for Dean to come back.

"Well, that rules him out," he said casually.

"Pardon?"

"It wasn't her dad that shot at us. I just asked her if he owned a gun, and he doesn't."

Amber groaned. "Do you honestly think she'd tell you?"

He sauntered on. "Well anyway, I made it clear we aren't put off that easily."

She stared at him. "Aren't we?"

"Nope… One way or another, we're taking a closer look at Lord Devlin's house, and no one is going to stop us." He shrugged. "And I told her so!"

Amber had the strangest feeling that letting the Blythes' daughter in on their plans wasn't the best thing they could have done.

It continued to worry her when she tried to get to sleep that night.

A tap-tapping on her bedroom door made her jump.

"Yes?"

Very slowly the handle turned and the door silently opened.

Amber sat bolt upright in bed, the duvet clutched under her chin. Heart thudding. Her eyes wide in the darkness of her room.

"Who is it?"

Dean stood in the doorway.

"Dean! You scared the life out of me!"

"Sorry. Can I come in?"

"What do you want?"

He put his finger to his lips and crept in. "I'm going back. You coming with me?"

"Back where?"

"The old house on the cliff. Obviously we're not going to get near it in the daytime, so we'll have to go at night… Well, you coming?"

"No I'm not!" she gasped. "It's dangerous enough when we could see where we were going – but in the dark!"

"I've borrowed Dad's torch; it's got a real strong light."

"No, it's too risky. It's pitch-black, we could

misjudge the edge of the cliff or…"

He shrugged. "Suit yourself, but I'm going."

"Wait!" she hissed, jumping out of bed.

The prospect of wandering all the way out to Lord Devlin's ramshackle house on the brink of the crumbling cliff at two in the morning was definitely a bad idea. But the thought of letting Dean go alone was even worse.

"Forget it. I'll go on my own."

She dragged her jeans on and pushed her feet into trainers. "I'll never sleep now. I'll be lying here waiting to see if you get back in one piece!"

He grinned. "Meet you downstairs in five minutes?"

"You're a real pain, you know that, Dean Brewster. And if we get grounded over this, I'm blaming you!"

"Know something, Amber?" Dean said with a grin.

"What?"

"You're the best cousin anyone ever had!"

Chapter 12

A huge silvery moon hung from the inky black sky, lighting their way across the deserted clifftop pathway. A chill, damp mist rolled in from the sea. Amber could taste it on her lips, feel its dampness in her hair.

Her thoughts strayed to that fateful night two hundred years ago when Lord Devlin had ridden across these clifftops, calling out to his wife through the storm. How easy it would be to misjudge the cliff edge and plunge over.

She shivered suddenly and pulled the sleeves of her sweater over her hands.

"You should have put a jacket on," said Dean. "The nights are always much colder when the day's been so hot."

"Thank you for the weather forecast! Did you bring the torch?"

"Sure did."

"Then how about switching it on? I really don't fancy falling over the cliff like poor old…" There was a click, and a bright yellow beam of light cut through the blackness, illuminating a contorted, grinning face.

"Waahhh!!" it shrieked.

Amber shrieked louder.

Dean's grin widened over the top of the light beam. "Scare you, did I?"

"You idiot!"

They walked on, cutting inland towards the style on to Farmer Draper's land.

"Hope he's not doing a night shift!" Amber remarked uneasily.

"He'll be sound asleep, come on."

The grass was wet with dew and mist. She shivered as the cold soaked through to her feet. It was as if all her senses were heightened. Her eyes were wide, watching for signs of anyone in the shadowy blackness – stalking them.

She could hear all the sounds of the night.

The ocean softly lapping against the shore. The whistling of the crickets. The rustling of grass.

But above all, what she could hear loudest was the thud-thudding of her heartbeat.

"Not much further," said Dean, swinging the torch from side to side in front of him.

"This is *not* a good idea!" she repeated, listening for other sounds. Like the sound of approaching footsteps. Or the sound of a shotgun being loaded. "We must be mad... Aaahh!" She screamed as something huge barred her way.

Something as big and solid as a brick wall. Only it wasn't a wall.

It moved – and breathed.

She pushed against it, panic-stricken. "Dean!"

She couldn't get past it. It seemed to be all around her, blocking her way. "Dean, help me!"

Suddenly two large eyes looked directly at her, luminous in the moonlight. She shrieked again.

"Amber, you idiot. It's just a cow!" cried

Dean, shining the torch at the surprised animal.

Her terror turned to fits of giggles, and she staggered against the huge, gentle animal and buried her face in its soft body. With a moo, it plodded away, leaving her almost collapsed with laughter.

"Shut up!" hissed Dean, "You'll wake someone."

"OK, OK," she said, controlling herself. The prospect of coming face to face with an angry farmer, looking down the barrel of a shotgun, had a swiftly sobering effect.

"Now keep quiet will you!" muttered Dean, walking on.

But Amber was still smiling to herself. "It scared the life out of me!"

"And you scared the life out of me. I nearly had a heart attack when you screamed."

"Well, if you'd been shining the torch properly, I'd have seen that cow before I bumped into it," said Amber, grabbing Dean's wrist to adjust the light from the torch.

For a second the yellow beam cut a large arc of light across the sky, silhouetting the eerie outline of trees.

And something else…

She froze, terror catching her breath.

"Dean…" she whispered. But no sound came.

Her nails dug into his wrist.

"Hey!"

Her heart was pounding. Beating against her ribcage as if it was trying to escape. But there was no escape – for anyone. It had seen them. Just as she had seen it, in the torchlight, a second ago.

"Get off my arm, Amber, I can shine a torch you know… What's the matter with you? You're as white as a…"

"Phantom!"

"What?"

"The ghost … him … Lord Devlin."

He looked incredulously at her. Then laughed. "Come off it. It was probably another cow."

Slowly she shook her head, her gaze riveted on the spot where she had seen it. "No…"

"Nice one, Amber, ten out of ten for acting ability. Now can we get going?"

"Lord Devlin," she breathed, her voice hushed in fear as the sensation of foreboding wrapped itself around her like a cold clammy blanket.

Dean struggled to prise her fingers from his arm, but they were locked in utter terror and her eyes were wild. "Come on, Amber, get a grip."

"Oh God, it's coming…"

The ground beneath their feet began to vibrate and shudder under the ferocity of galloping hooves. The thudding rang in her ears.

Dean heard it too then. There was fear in his voice as he cried out. "Amber … what's that? What is it?"

"Run!" she screamed.

But it was too late.

From out of the darkness a white stallion came hurtling at them through a cloud of dust.

And seated astride the powerful beast sat its rider.

A rider in a black velvet cape that flapped and billowed out like a shroud.

A faceless rider.

Hideous.

For where his face should have been, were the dry parched white bones of a skull!

Chapter 13

Amber wanted to run. With all her heart she wanted to run away from this awful apparition. But terror had struck her rigid.

Dean, too, was rooted to the spot, too shocked to move.

A flurry of cold air and dust gusted into their faces as the stallion shuddered to a halt just metres away from them. It reared up on its powerful hind legs, its front feet pawing the air, steam rising from its flanks.

Through the cloud of thick, choking dust Amber could feel the heat from the ghostly animal. She could hear the flap of velvet from the phantom rider's cape. And all the while his black hollow eyes bore down on them – terrifying … haunting.

Fighting against her terror she dragged at her cousin's arm and yelled, "Run, Dean! Run as fast as you can!"

They raced away, feet barely touching the ground. Across the fields, stumbling, tripping, dragging themselves up and running again. Running until their legs screamed out in agony.

They didn't stop until they were back at the outskirts of the town.

Dean doubled up in pain. "I'm going to be sick!"

Amber collapsed against a garden wall, gasping for breath. She peered back through the blackness. There was no sign of him – Lord Devlin, the phantom.

Just a black void, like the awful blackness of his eyes.

"I wouldn't have believed it," she said, gasping. "If I hadn't seen it with my own eyes."

Dean gulped in huge lungfuls of air. "To tell you the truth, I've never believed in that legend, I was just winding you up..." He stared at her, fear still there in his eyes. "But it's true! All those stories about his ghost haunting the clifftops are true!"

"And it was so *real*," whispered Amber. "I thought ghosts were supposed to be misty, floaty images. That horse seemed like real flesh and blood. You could feel the ground vibrating. I could even smell it!"

"I know," murmured Dean, his eyes wild and staring. "I thought it was going to trample us into the ground. I thought it wanted to kill us!"

She threaded her arm through his for support. He was shaking. "Come on, let's go home."

He looked miserable. "Sorry, Amber. This is all my fault."

She tried to smile. "We're safe now, Dean, that's all that matters. We're safe."

But as they walked back home through the dark shadowy streets, Amber had never felt less safe in her life.

Chapter 14

Amber eventually got to sleep, but awoke suddenly to the sound of something flapping.

The phantom's cape!

She sat bolt upright in bed, eyes huge, heart pounding.

But there was no one.

No phantom – nothing. Just her curtain flapping at the open window in the warm morning breeze.

As the terrors of the night gradually faded, making it all seem like a terrible nightmare, she slipped out of bed.

It was another hot day. Already the sun was high in the sky and she dressed in shorts and T-shirt and went down for breakfast.

Everyone was up and dashing about getting ready for work. Dean cast her a warning glance over the top of his cornflakes.

"Don't tell them," he whispered. "We'll both be grounded if they find out we went out in the night."

"What are you pair whispering about?" Uncle Dave frowned, watching them through the mirror as he straightened his collar.

"Nothing," Amber answered, avoiding his eyes. She tucked into a breakfast she really couldn't face, aware that her uncle was giving them both curious looks.

At the first opportunity, she and Dean went out and headed towards town – away from the cliff tops.

"Did you sleep?" Amber asked.

"Not much. Did you?"

"A bit." She glanced over her shoulder in the direction of the cliffs. "I wonder if he's still out there."

Dean shuddered. "Shut up will you, it gives me the creeps just thinking about it."

They walked on in silence, towards the promenade already teeming with holidaymakers. Dean's mood perked up as the noisy, bustling atmosphere of the arcades and fairground engulfed them.

Amber remained lost in her thoughts, saddened to think that the spirit of poor Lord Devlin was still so tormented that it was stuck here in a world he had no part of.

"Hey – look who's over there!" Dean suddenly said, digging her in the ribs. "It's her again ... the Blythes' daughter. Come on..."

"Oh no," Amber groaned. "Dean, come back!"

He turned, half jogging backwards so that only Amber could hear him. "I meant to ask her last night why her parents were burning pictures of her grandparents, only I never got a chance. Gonna ask her now."

"Oh sure," Amber muttered, following reluctantly. "And she might just tell us to mind our own business."

The girl was eating candyfloss. Dean caught up with her and pinched a chunk of fluffy pink candy, popping it cheekily into his mouth.

"Ta!"

Amber cringed, but to her amazement the girl actually smiled at Dean. And by the time Amber had dawdled up to join them, they were chatting away like old friends.

"Hey, Amber, this is Nina, you remember her, don't you? She lives out at Hazelfield Lodge."

Nina turned her head to look directly into Amber's face: it had a discomforting effect, unfriendly, questioning – suspicious.

"Hello," Amber murmured.

Nina Blythe made no reply – except to Dean. "I'm going on the roller-coaster. Coming?"

He pulled a face. "No cash, sorry."

"I'll pay," Nina said, tossing her half-eaten candyfloss on to the ground at Amber's feet.

"There is a bin…" Amber began, but Nina Blythe was already striding through the crowds towards the roller-coaster with Dean hot at her heels.

With a sigh Amber followed, realizing that not only did she have a troublesome cousin to watch out for, but a spoilt rich kid too.

The queue for the roller-coaster wasn't too long, and as they shuffled forward, Amber decided to try and find out more about Nina's grandparents – seeing as Dean seemed to have totally forgotten what their aim was.

"Sorry to hear about your grandparents, Nina," Amber said, as they inched up the wooden steps on to the platform of the ride.

For a second a vague look crossed the girl's face, then she shrugged. "Yes, that was a bit of a shame. I quite liked them."

Amber and Dean exchanged glances, then Amber continued, "How did they die? A road accident or something?"

"Yes, that's right. A car accident... Dean, let's try and get in the first carriage. I love being at the front."

"Me too..." He hesitated and looked at Amber. "Unless you sit with Nina and I'll sit behind."

Nina gave Amber no time to agree or disagree. "No way! I'm paying, so I get to say who I'm sitting next to. And I'm sitting next to you, Dean." She cast a cold and calculating smile back over her shoulder at Amber.

"Sit where you like," said Amber, thinking how alike Nina and her mother were. Both unpleasant. "And I've got my own money thanks."

"Suit yourself," Nina said dismissively.

As they neared the front of the queue, the excitement of the ride made Amber nervous. The thundering, noisy carriages hurtled along the platform, emptying its breathless passengers only to refill and take the next victims on its twisting, spiralling, breath-taking ride.

Nevertheless, she hadn't forgotten what she wanted to talk to Nina Blythe about.

"So what happened exactly?" Amber persisted. "To your grandparents – how did the accident happen?"

Nina swung round, her face was pinched and angry at being questioned. "Does it matter? They're dead and that's all there is to it!"

Ignoring her outburst, Amber went on, keenly gauging the girl's reactions. "Did you know your parents have burnt all their photographs?"

She flinched, slightly. "So?"

"So it's a funny thing to do. People don't just destroy precious photographs, especially of their parents and grandparents!"

The carriages of the roller-coaster emptied, ready for them. And as they climbed aboard, Amber continued her questioning. "I thought it was really strange…"

"They didn't get on, all right!" Nina snapped, as she took her front seat next to Dean. "Now would you shut up about them!"

Metal arms came automatically down and locked them into their seats. Amber's heart began to thud as with a rumble of wheels and machinery, the carriage moved forward, gathering speed, climbing the steep track to the very top, where the rails disappeared leaving a sheer, almost vertical, drop.

They hurtled downwards.

Amber clung on and squeezed her eyes tightly shut as they whizzed along the track.

The sound of screaming filled her ears.

And then they were slowing again. Climbing. The wheels click-clicking on the track. She opened her eyes. They were incredibly high.

So high that she could see right over the funfair and beyond ... to the cliff tops.

She found herself scanning the horizon ... looking for him – the phantom.

She shivered.

And then, suddenly, the carriage dipped at a terrifying angle and they sped down the track, the wind snatching away her breath, making her forget everything for a few moments except the thrill of the ride.

Finally they hurtled along the platform and came to a bone-jarring halt.

They scrambled off.

"That was brilliant!" Dean gasped, clinging on to Amber as his knees buckled.

Amber gave a relieved laugh. "I'm just glad it's over. That was scary!"

Nina turned to Amber. "You were asking how my grandparents died ... it wasn't a car accident at all ... it was a fairground ride. Similar to this one actually. A carriage came off the track and smashed into them as they were walking along. It flattened them." Her mouth twisted cruelly. "Satisfied? Anyway, I'm going again – anyone else coming?"

Dean's eyes lit up as if he couldn't believe his luck. "You bet... Amber?"

Amber said nothing. She didn't believe a word of Nina's explanation. The girl was sick.

"Well, Amber, you coming?"

Amber shook her head. Not sure exactly what she couldn't stomach at the moment, another ride, or being anywhere near Nina Blythe.

After a second and third go on the roller-coaster, Nina dragged Dean along to the pirate ship and the waltzers and almost every other stomach-churning ride on the funfair. Amber tagged along at a distance, feeling like a spare part.

They ended up in the amusement arcade where Nina changed a five-pound note into coins. Amber saw the look on Dean's face and dragged him to one side. "She's got more money than she knows what to do with!"

He grinned. "I know, great, isn't it?"

"No, it's ridiculous. Where does she get it all from anyway?"

"Rich parents!" Dean remarked with a mischievous wink. And hurried back to join his new friend.

Amber followed him, growing more and more irritated. "Dean, I think it's time we were getting back…"

"No way! I'm going to show Nina how to cheat on the avalanche game in a minute."

"No, don't, you'll get into trouble. Look, I really think it's time that we went back."

"Bye!" Nina said, coldly. Not looking at Amber, just feeding coin after coin into the jangling machine.

Amber stared at the backs of their heads. Then, angrily, she swung away. She'd had enough. They were welcome to each other.

She spent the afternoon sunbathing alone in her aunt and uncle's back garden. The glorious sunshine combined with her restless night made her sleepy.

She dozed off, thinking of phantoms and fairgrounds and two elderly smiling faces that turned black and charred before her eyes.

It was an unpleasant sleep and she awoke to the sensation of someone bending over her, blocking out the sunlight, forming a dark shadow over her.

She blinked open her eyes, the nightmare fading only to be replaced by something far worse.

A face hovered just inches above her.

A hideous face.

White and wrinkled with an ugly hooked nose and rotting teeth. Straggly grey wisps of hair trailed from his balding head and tickled her cheeks.

Amber screamed.

Chapter 15

He didn't disappear as nightmares should. He remained, hovering inches above her, vile and hideous.

He started to laugh!

Amber recognized that laugh.

She also recognized the T-shirt and shorts the ugly old man was wearing. And she would know those spindly legs anywhere.

"Dean!" she cried, jumping up and thumping him.

He peeled off the rubber mask and leapt about the garden, laughing. "Gotcha!"

"You pig! You nearly gave me heart failure!"

"Great, isn't it?" he grinned. "Got it from

the joke shop on the promenade. They've got all sorts of masks like this and jokes and tricks and things. Here, try one of these sweets!"

"No thanks, I don't particularly want my mouth to turn blue or to blow soap bubbles. Anyway I thought you hadn't any money."

He wiggled his eyebrows. "Nina bought them for me, and the mask."

"I might have known. And I bet she suggested you try and scare me to death with it."

"Nah! That was my idea."

Amber cast him a disbelieving look. "Nothing would surprise me about that girl."

"She's OK, she's good fun."

"Everyone's entitled to their own opinion," she said stiffly as she folded up her sun bed. "Are you going to the fair again with her tomorrow?"

He looked disappointed. "Nope, I dropped a few hints, but she said she had to do some work at home."

"Another clear-out?" mused Amber. "I think that is so strange – destroying her grand-parents' photographs."

"Don't blame Nina for that," said Dean defensively. "It was her parents who did it, not her. She probably didn't know anything about it till you mentioned it."

"Didn't you get any more information out of her?"

"Didn't get a chance. I told her about the phantom though, only she didn't believe a word of it. Thought I was making it all up."

"I wouldn't have believed it myself if it hadn't happened to me," she murmured, shivering at the mention of the phantom. "Anyway, what shall we do tomorrow? And don't suggest we go poking about around the old house, because I'm never *ever* going anywhere near that place again!"

"May as well go down to Slipper Bay. This hot weather can't last much longer. Weather forecast predicts storms are looming."

Amber shielded her eyes against the sunshine as she looked up into the cloudless blue sky.

Storms? She didn't think so.

Chapter 16

The following morning brought another glorious day. Not a cloud in the sky and the sun hotter than ever. A day on the beach was precisely the thing.

But she was hot and sweating by the time they reached Slipper Bay. She couldn't wait to change into her swimming costume and cool off in the sea.

It was refreshingly cold, and the sun's rays sparkled and glinted on the waves, dazzling her. But she was aware too of the steep curve of the ocean's bed. Warning her that she would soon be out of her depth if she waded too far out.

Dean seemed to have the same thought.

As he floated towards her, bobbing about like a cork, he said, "Nearly forgot to warn you, you mustn't get out of your depth. There's some dangerous tides and currents just a bit further out. If you got sucked out to sea here, you'd never be seen again. Remember Lord Devlin? If he hadn't got tangled up in some fishing boat's nets they'd never have got his body back."

A chill ran through her. The sea suddenly lost its charm. Suddenly it seemed deadly – dangerous. As if it were lulling her into a false sense of security before dragging her away – to her death.

She headed for shore, wading out as quickly as she could. Panicking a little as the current pulled her back, making her escape slow and difficult.

"Hey, where you going?" Dean yelled.

"I've had enough – you coming?"

"May as well," he grumbled, wading out after her.

As they walked up the beach, he pointed to the far end of the Bay, where the cliffs jutted out on a peninsular. "Looks pretty spectacular from this angle, don't you think?"

Amber gazed far off, at the house hanging precariously on the brink of the cliff. The area directly below had been fenced off, keeping people away from the danger zone.

But it wasn't the old house that troubled her.

"What are we going to do, Dean?" she asked quietly.

"Do about what?"

"Lord Devlin."

For a second Dean was silent, then he exploded into a half laugh, half gasp. "We can't *do* anything about him – he's dead, Amber. He's been dead for two hundred years!"

She pushed her hair back from her eyes. "But it's so tragic ... he's still searching for his wife. And he'll go on searching for her – for ever."

"Just as well if you ask me," Dean remarked, drying himself.

"Why?"

"Well, I mean, *he* didn't look too hot, did he – lost a bit of weight I reckon. And she's not going to look much better! I reckon it's best if they never clap eyes on each other."

She flicked him with her towel. "Oh you are so gross, Dean Brewster!"

He dodged aside, laughing. "He was all skin and bone. A bag of chips wouldn't do him any harm."

Ignoring him, she spread out her towel on the burning sand and sat down.

The hot breeze had already dried her skin, leaving it feeling prickly hot. And the scorching breeze had a discomforting effect. It was too hot, too sultry. Perhaps Dean was right about the storm.

Something was coming – if not today, then tomorrow, or the day after.

With a sigh, she took her sketch pad and pencils from her bag.

"What you going to draw?"

"You'll see," she murmured, finding a clean page.

It was easy to conjure up the powerful image that had imprinted itself on to her brain – that magnificent white horse rearing up on its hind legs, steam rising from its back.

The black gaping eyes of Lord Devlin, his velvet cape billowing out in the wind.

Not at all like she imagined a ghost would be – misty, unreal. The ghost of Lord Devlin was as real and solid as any living thing.

For a while Dean watched, then, growing bored, he headed off towards the rocks and rock pools at the base of the cliffs.

Amber worked intensely, oblivious to everything else. As she shaded in the muscle structure of the horse she called out: "Dean, how come the ghost of Lord Devlin appears as a skull yet his horse is still in one piece?"

"How do I know… Hey, I've found a crab!"

Amber got on with her drawing, glancing up occasionally to see her cousin exploring the rock pools, or wading in the shallows of the sea. But her concentration was solely on her drawing.

As the sun drifted across the pale blue sky, the rays reflected up off her sketch pad, making her eyes heavy and her eyelids droop.

Finally, she pushed her artwork aside and lay her head down on a folded towel. Sleep crept up on her like a warm silky shadow.

From somewhere far, far away, she heard Dean talking to her. "If you're going to sleep, Amber, cover up or you'll get sunburnt."

"Mmm," she murmured sleepily.

Vaguely she felt a beach towel being draped over her. It was cool against her skin, shielding her from the merciless sun overhead.

She slept soundly.

High above, the sun moved slowly across the sky, sweeping away the pale azure and colouring it a darker, deeper blue.

A stormy blue.

The tide turned.

The waves suddenly rose with a disturbing urgency. As if they could no longer play and dance with the carefreeness of morning. Now they had a purpose.

And they turned and rolled steadily towards the beach.

Chapter 17

Amber stirred in her sleep as the breeze stiffened, fluttering the pages of her sketch pad.

The fluttering crept into her dreams, becoming the sound of a black velvet cape flapping in the wind.

She awoke with a start.

Her heart was thudding. For a second she thought the sound was of hoof beats pounding across the beach. Alarmed, she sat bolt upright, squinting her eyes into focus.

Slowly, as she came fully awake, the sound faded.

The tide was coming in. Already half the beach was covered in churning, foaming water. And the hot breeze seemed to have blown the sun out of the sky, leaving behind a heavy foreboding deep blue.

In the distance, black storm clouds crawled over the horizon.

"You're right, Dean, there is a storm brewing... Dean?" She looked around, there was no sign of him. "Dean!"

No reply.

"Dean ... Dean, where are you?"

She wandered up and down the beach, calling his name, but the roar of the ocean snatched her shouts away and tossed them out to sea.

She felt her throat tighten. Dean wouldn't have just left her, not with the tide coming in. He wouldn't! He had to be around here somewhere.

She ran to the water's edge, to where the frothy waves melted into the gritty sand. She scanned the water's surface for him swimming out there.

But there was no sign.

Panic made a knot in her stomach and she ran back along the beach, searching around the rock pools, in case he had slipped, and was lying hurt somewhere.

"Dean! Where are you?"

The wind was gathering force, whipping the storm clouds nearer to shore. Amber called out his name until her throat ached. "Dean! Dean, answer me!"

But the only reply was the mournful cry of the black-headed gulls overhead.

Suddenly she was afraid – afraid for Dean. He must have gone swimming and got into difficulties – the undercurrents were treacherous here, he'd said so himself…

She had to get help.

She threw everything into her bag and then, just as she turned to run for help, something caught her eye.

A tiny speck of red against the black slipper clay of the cliffs, far along the coast, close to the area fenced off.

Someone was scrambling up the cliff near the old house. Someone in a red T-shirt and shorts. Someone who looked remarkably like Dean.

"You idiot!" she muttered, nevertheless

relieved that he hadn't drowned.

She threw her bag over her shoulder and headed towards him. But her relief swiftly turned to anger. How could he be so stupid? Those cliffs were treacherous!

The golden strip of beach was growing narrower as she trudged along. White-capped waves swept into froth around her feet, making the pebbles sing. Cold water refilled the rock pools.

Some distance out to sea a small, blue motor boat bobbed about on the waves, but as she got closer, she saw it was unmanned and anchored.

Her heart sank. She'd hoped there would be a fisherman on board – someone who could help if Dean fell.

He was almost at the top of the cliff – on the other side of the fence the council had put up to keep people out of danger. Obviously they hadn't accounted for Dean!

She watched him clawing and picking his way up, his feet sending showers of dirt rolling down on to the beach.

She called his name, but he didn't hear.

And then, clinging on to the overhanging shrubbery, he hauled himself to the top and disappeared from view.

"Dean!" she shouted at the top of her voice. But the wind took the sound away, and she was left at the bottom, suddenly feeling very alone.

And afraid.

A glance back along the beach increased her alarm. The tide was almost at the sloping rockfall where they had come down to Slipper Bay. She doubted there was time to walk back and get up before the water became too deep.

If she tried and didn't make it, she would be cut off by the incoming tide. The cliffs were steep further back. This was the only place where they sloped enough to scramble up.

For long agonizing moments she considered the two options.

To try and race against the incoming tide – or to climb a dangerous crumbling cliff.

Neither choice filled her with joy!

Chapter 18

The speed the waves rolled up the beach made Amber's decision for her.

She would have to climb.

With a deep, determined breath, she secured her bag on her back and looked around to see how Dean had got through the fence.

It wasn't difficult, there were gaps everywhere. Obviously the workmen had assumed people wouldn't want to walk beneath a house that was ready to fall on them at any minute!

She heaved a sigh. They *definitely* hadn't accounted for Dean – or her!

She scrambled through one of the gaps.

The rock felt soft to her touch, more like

earth than stone. It crumbled as she climbed, sending showers of black dirt cascading downwards. But at least it made good hand- and footholds even if it did turn her fingernails black.

The cliff face was steep but not sheer, and she was able to hang on to the fencing that ran a good way up the cliff.

But the higher she climbed, the less confident she became. The beach looked a long way down from here. And the hot wind gusted against her, threatening to blow her off the cliff.

With a thudding heart, she clawed her way up, inch by inch, towards the summit.

With hands, elbows and knees that were black from the clay, she scrambled on. Climbing higher and higher.

Her long hair streamed around her head, blocking her vision, while gulls screeched out angrily that people were invading their domain.

At last, Amber was able to reach out and grasp the roots and vines from the shrubbery dangling over the cliff edge. Slowly, with arms that trembled from the exertion, she managed to haul herself on to flat land.

She flopped there for a while, getting her breath back, quite pleased with her achievement.

She was directly beside Lord Devlin's house, close to where the barbed wire had been cut.

"Dean … Dean, are you there?"

Amber guessed what his intention was – to get into the old house the back way without alerting Farmer Draper or anyone else who might want to take a pot-shot at him.

Not to mention the phantom!

"Dean … answer me!"

But only the whistle of the wind and the cry of gulls answered her.

She tiptoed over the egg-shelled ground and squeezed through the opening in the barbed wire. Nervously she pushed against the back door.

It opened.

The door creaked on rusted hinges, allowing a beam of light to cut through the stale darkness. The stench of something rotting wafted out, almost making her sick. But she pinched her nose and crept in.

It was cold.

The chill seeped through her thin clothing and sent shivers through her body.

She walked nervously through the kitchen with its black cast-iron cooking range and massive fireplace, and battered copper pans that dangled from hooks high in the cracked walls. A door led into a huge hallway.

It was breathtaking.

The floor was mosaic marble tiles. A wide sweeping staircase stretched up to an upstairs balcony. Beside it was a long stained-glass window – boarded up from the outside and coated in decades of cobwebs on the inside. And a magnificent chandelier that hung down from the ornate ceiling.

Amber gasped at the faded, neglected beauty. It had been a beautiful house, and, she guessed, a happy home for Lord Devlin and Isabella – for a while at least.

Doors led off at all angles from the hallway; she peeped into each, searching for Dean. Everywhere had been stripped bare, the treasures and trappings of the home long gone.

There were no paintings that she could see.

She stood at the foot of the stairs. "Dean! Are you up there?"

She was half afraid to shout too loud in case she disturbed the fragile ground beneath the house's foundations.

But there was no reply from Dean. Just the creaks and groans of old timber and the wail of the wind that whistled through the cracks.

But she couldn't turn back now without looking upstairs. Dean might have got himself trapped up there somehow.

And there was another reason for taking a peep upstairs. Perhaps that's where the last of Isabella's paintings were hiding.

The wind outside seemed to be growing fiercer, blustering against the wooden panels at the window, making the glass rattle. And Dean's words suddenly jumped into her head.

The next storm should probably take the house over the cliff. Hope I'm around to see it.

Amber hoped she wasn't!

The staircase creaked under her feet, the

wood seeming to bend under her weight. From the corner of her eye she glimpsed a spider scuttling back amongst the cobwebs.

The top landing was in shadow. But she could make out the doors leading off from the corridor.

She peered into each room.

"Dean, are you in here?"

Up here a few old treasures remained. An old chest of drawers, a water jug and bowl. In another room there was a bed.

But the smell was worse up here.

A sweet, sickening smell, like rotting meat.

She tried not to dwell on the fact that she was high up in a house that was teetering on the brink of a cliff.

The very thought made her feel giddy, light-headed.

She pressed on, determined to see every room – just in case Dean *was* here.

Just in case a collection of Isabella's paintings had been left.

Another bedroom revealed a pile of junk bundled up in a corner – some wooden crates, a couple of old carpets rolled up.

But in here, the smell was almost unbearable. She guessed the carpets must have rotted.

And then she saw them!

Her heart missed a beat.

On the wall behind the junk hung three oil paintings!

Amber couldn't believe her luck.

Eagerly she clambered over the junk to get a better look in the gloom of the bedroom. There was a name signed in the corner of the paintings... She tried to get closer, standing on top of one of the bulky rolled-up carpets so that she could see.

But her foot slipped.

The carpet unrolled a little, and something that had been bound up inside the carpet, slipped out.

It scratched against Amber's leg and she looked down.

Terror engulfed her – hot suffocating terror.

She couldn't breathe. Sweat broke out all over her skin. Nausea welled up in her throat and her eyes bulged as she stared down at the *thing* that had scratched against her leg.

A hand!

Grey and rotting, and crawling with maggots.

A short, thick fingernail had made a thin red scratch down her leg.

She let out a strangled cry of horror, then pressed her hand over her mouth to stop herself being sick.

She could see part of the arm, clad in a man's shirt. The rest of the body was still rolled in the carpet.

She backed away ... backed out of the room, her eyes riveted on the vile, sickening sight.

Then she turned and ran.

Along the passageway, stumbling down the stairs, across the hall and through the kitchen.

Fresh air and daylight made her gasp.

She forced through the barbed wire, leaving half of her T-shirt on the sharp points without even noticing.

Horror and terror made her oblivious to everything.

Everything except that fact that she had just discovered a dead body.

Chapter 19

Outside, the storm clouds had rolled by. The sun was out again. Amber didn't notice, she ran blindly across the meadows, her hair streaming out behind her.

So blinded by fear that she didn't spot the man hurrying towards her, until he had caught her arm and swung her to a stop.

Under his arm was a shotgun.

"Let me go!" she screamed, pulling away from him.

"Hey now, hold your horses young lady, what's the big hurry?"

It was the farmer. She recognized him as the man she had seen the other day, just before someone shot at them.

The dead person could have been shot dead!

"Well, what's the trouble, you came haring across the field like a frightened rabbit."

She couldn't tell him ... he could be the murderer!

And she wasn't in any state to make up excuses.

"Let me go."

Throwing his hand off her, she broke free and ran on ... across the stile, along the cliff path, exhausted but too afraid to stop.

Then, in the distance, she saw Dean. He looked frantic. Nina was with him, and they were pacing back and forth across the clifftop, peering down, shouting something.

As she got nearer, she heard what they were shouting – her name.

He thought she was still on the beach!

"Dean!" she cried and he swung round.

"Amber!"

Nina pulled a face. "See, I told you she'd be all right."

Dean raced up to her. "God, Amber, I've been worried sick. I lost track of time. I went for a climb; when I got to the top and looked down and saw how the tide had come in I nearly died. I went charging back across the cliff tops to get back and wake you, only the tide was in – right where you'd been sleeping."

Amber couldn't speak.

All she could do was cling on to her cousin's arms for support.

"Amber … you OK?"

"There's a body … in the house … a dead body."

"What!"

Nina raised her eyebrows. "What *is* she talking about?"

"I went in," she gasped. "Went upstairs – looking for you – and there was a body rolled up in a carpet." Bile rose in her throat again. "Dean, it was crawling with maggots!"

"Oh gross!" Nina groaned, pulling a face. "You will excuse me if I don't hang around, only it might put me off my dinner."

She walked off, leaving Amber and Dean staring at each other.

"A body!" Dean exclaimed in disbelief.

She nodded. "It was horrible. Oh Dean, it must be murder, people don't just die and roll themselves up in carpets. Someone murdered that person and hid the body."

"Who was it? Could you see its face?"

"No, just an arm and a hand."

"Someone young or old … man or woman?"

"I don't know," she cried helplessly. "Oldish I think and it might have been a man's arm, but I don't know for sure, I couldn't tell."

"Are you sure?"

She felt like shaking him. "Of course I'm sure. It was a dead body!"

For a moment he looked thoughtful, then he took her arm. "Come on, we'll go and tell my dad. He'll investigate it, he'll sort it all out."

Amber wanted to run all the way to the police and blurt out what she'd discovered, but she was exhausted and her legs would only drag her to the police station at the far end of town at a snail's pace.

The station sergeant suggested they sat in

the waiting room until someone could take her statement. No one seemed in any hurry and after sitting for ages, impatiently drumming her fingers, Amber was called to the sergeant's desk.

She had never known anyone write so slowly!

By the time they left the police station, she felt like screaming. "He didn't believe me!"

"Course he did, he'll send someone out to investigate."

"Yes, but when?" Amber demanded, totally frustrated.

Dean shrugged. "What's the rush? A dead body isn't going to go far, is it!"

It was late when Uncle Dave arrived home from his shift. Amber and Dean had waited up for him, anxious to know what had happened, and if they'd found out who'd been murdered and how.

But Uncle Dave was strangely subdued and he and Aunt Joan talked quietly in the kitchen for some minutes before he sat down in his armchair.

Amber and Dean stared eagerly at him.

"Well, who was it, how did he die?" Dean finally blurted out.

Uncle Dave eyed them both curiously. "You did say the old house on the cliff?"

"Yes, in an upstairs room – the one at the end of the corridor – in the carpet..." Amber saw his expression, and a sinking feeling crept over her.

Aunt Joan stood behind her husband. Silently.

Amber frowned. "What's wrong – who was it?"

Uncle Dave took a deep breath. "Amber, I don't know what you and Dean are playing at..."

The sinking sensation in the pit of her stomach worsened. "Pardon?"

"But if this is some kind of practical joke..."

Her head began to swim. "A joke..."

"All right, a mistake then. But whatever it was you think you saw, believe me, it was not a dead body."

"It was!" she cried, leaping up. "I saw it!"

"I don't think so, Amber," Uncle Dave said

sternly. "A number of valuable officers went out to investigate. And there was no dead body rolled up in a carpet. There weren't even any carpets."

"But there must have been," she cried, confusion making her eyes water. "You didn't look in the right room…"

"We looked in *every* room," Uncle Dave said sternly. "And believe me, Amber. There is no dead body!"

Chapter 20

Everyone was staring at her – even Dean. "What was it then?" she demanded, anger and confusion making her voice tremble.

"Nothing!" Uncle Dave said quietly. "Like I've just said, there was no dead body, no carpet, no paintings..."

"No paintings either?" she gasped.

Uncle Dave continued. "Admittedly the house was exactly like you described it. I've no doubts that you went inside it ... which is probably the most foolhardy thing you could ever have done. Don't you realize how dangerous that house is?"

Amber's head was reeling, spinning... No dead body?

But there was!

She'd seen it, touched it – smelt it…

"The smell!" she cried excitedly. "You must have smelt it … a sweet, sickly rotting smell."

"The place did have an unpleasant odour," he agreed. "But the house has been standing empty for years. It's hardly going to smell fresh, is it?"

Amber turned desperately to Dean.

He looked helpless. "You must have been mistaken, Amber."

She felt like screaming. "Mistaken! It was the most vile thing I've ever seen. Do you think I could have imagined that!"

Aunt Joan put an arm around her shoulder. "Amber, love … you'd been asleep on the beach under that hot sun. You woke up and couldn't find Dean – that must have been traumatic for you. Then you had to climb a cliff to get away from the incoming tide…" She smiled kindly. "Love, you probably didn't know what you were doing."

"I'm not crazy if that's what you're getting at!" Amber shouted. "I saw a body … an arm. Someone has been murdered. I didn't imagine it!"

"I'll make you some tea," said Aunt Joan. "And then an early night."

"Why won't you listen to me? I didn't imagine it. I didn't!"

"Now calm down," said Uncle Dave. "There's no point getting yourself all upset. And I think Joan's right. Get yourself off to bed and she'll bring you a cup of tea and something to eat. You've had a touch of sunstroke, I reckon... Joan best ring the doctor. Too much sun can cause hallucinations."

Amber's head swam.

Was it possible that they were right and she was wrong? Could she have imagined it?

Her head began to throb and she was glad of Aunt Joan's steadying arm as she went up to bed.

Her aunt placed a cold damp cloth on her head as she lay down.

"Aunty Joan, I did see an arm, it was crawling with maggots."

"I know," she said kindly. "Now try and rest."

Amber was left lying on her bed in a

darkened room. Outside her bedroom door, her aunt and uncle whispered to each other.

"What's upset me most," whispered Uncle Dave, "is that a team of police officers had to go and investigate her claim. They had to go through the house, aware that it could go over the cliff at any moment. She put all their lives in danger."

"It wasn't her fault, Dave," soothed Aunt Joan. "She was hallucinating. She's got sunstroke. It probably *was* real to her."

Uncle Dave sounded doubtful. "I don't know. I thought the idea of having her stay here was to keep Dean out of mischief. I reckon she could be more trouble than she's worth."

Amber rolled over and curled herself into a ball to shut out the world.

She'd imagined it! How could her mind play such an awful trick on her?

She wrapped her arms around her knees, as tears began to sting her eyes.

Her hand brushed against her leg and she winced as she touched a sore scratch on her leg. At first she ignored it. She'd got a few painful scratches on her arms from where she'd dashed through the barbed wire.

Only then she remembered … that had been where she'd thought the dead person's fingernail had caught her.

She threw back the duvet and turned on her bedside lamp.

The thin red line was quite visible even in the pale light from her lamp.

Her heart thudded.

Imagination? Hallucinations?

No!

That scratch hadn't been caused by barbed wire.

That scratch had been caused by the fingernail on a dead person's hand!

Chapter 21

"Are you sure you're all right?" Aunt Joan fretted the following morning.

"I'm fine," Amber assured her. "And I'm sorry about causing so much trouble yesterday. You were right, I think I had too much sun."

Aunt Joan brushed the hair from Amber's eyes. "You have to be careful, the weather at the moment is so hot. I'm afraid we're in for an almighty storm before much longer."

"Better take your umbrella then," Amber joked, as she followed her aunt to the door.

They both looked up at the glorious blue sky.

"Not today I don't think," said her aunt. "Looks like another scorcher. See you later."

Amber waved her goodbye and then closed the door, her smile dissolving as she leant against the door, her thoughts racing.

Someone *had* been murdered. Murdered and left to rot in that old house. Probably the murderer was waiting for the right moment to get rid of the body, but because of her discovering it, they'd had to move fast.

But who ... who could have known?

Farmer Draper! Of course! She'd bumped into him close to the house ... if he was the guilty one he would have guessed.

No wonder he'd shot at them the other day. He had a very good reason for keeping them away from Lord Devlin's house!

But then another thought jumped into her head.

Farmer Draper wasn't the only person she'd bumped into yesterday.

There had been someone else...

Nina Blythe!

Amber left the house early, walking purposefully down to Slipper Bay. She had discovered a murder and no one believed her. The police had no intention of doing anything about it. So that meant just one thing.

She would have to get to the bottom of this herself.

The cliff paths were deserted as she walked along. Her only companions were the seagulls that swooped and cried overhead.

She wasn't sure what she was doing, except it seemed sensible to return to the scene of the crime, and see if she could find a clue ... something ... anything.

After clambering down on to the sands, she took off her trainers and waded along in the shallows, enjoying the cold fresh water frothing around her ankles. The tide was right out now and the beach sands cold and wet.

She walked along, towards the fenced-off part of the beach, beneath the house. The little boat bobbed about on the water, a long way out.

Amber frowned.

The boat had been moored further out yesterday. Even taking into account the tides, the boat was anchored in a different place.

Someone had been out in it.

At some time between yesterday afternoon

and this morning, someone had taken the boat out and brought it back. At the same time a dead body had been removed from the old house.

"*There's some dangerous tides and currents just a bit further out*," Dean had said. "*If you got sucked out to sea here, you'd never be seen again*."

Amber stared at the innocent little boat. Had it been used to take the body way out and then to dump it into the sea – to be sucked down, and never seen again?

Her gaze shifted up the beach. It was a straight line up to the house. A body secured inside a rolled-up carpet could have been lowered down the cliff … someone slowly lowering it by rope … someone clambering down with it, easing it over the rocks.

She walked briskly along the beach towards the sloping wall of black slipper clay. Reaching the fence she looked up at the cliff face she'd climbed yesterday. On the lower slopes, everything had been washed clean and smooth by the tide. But higher up, out of reach of rising water, there were marks in the black earth. Holes, made by hands and feet, and a wide smooth track, as if something had slid down.

She shivered, picturing the scene of someone lowering a dead body down that cliff.

They must have been strong.

Farmer Draper looked strong, but Nina wasn't… But Nina together with her parents…

Her stomach tightened.

Was the dead body connected with the photographs the Blythes were destroying? And those clothes they gave away – could they have been the clothes of the dead person?

Had they murdered someone and were getting rid of all the evidence?

Her heart suddenly missed a beat. They had got rid of two lots of clothing – a man's and a woman's. They had destroyed photographs of a man and a woman.

An image suddenly flashed into Amber's head, and her knees buckled.

That bedroom – up there in the old house. The pile of junk that she had clambered over to try and see Isabella's paintings. The rolled-up carpet that had a dead body inside it…

Only it wasn't just one roll of carpet. There had been two!

Two rolled-up carpets.

Her skin began to crawl. Could that have meant two dead bodies?

The man and woman in the photographs ... Jeremy Blythe's parents!

Amber sank down on to the sands, the horror of it all washing over her like crashing waves.

And she suddenly knew, without a doubt, that there hadn't been just one murder – there had been two!

There was a double-murderer at large ... and they knew that she was on to them.

Another more terrifying thought struck her.

If the Blythes *were* killers ... if they were so evil that they'd murdered members of their own family and gone to so much trouble to cover up their tracks, were they likely to let Amber go around telling people what she'd seen?

Wouldn't it be easier and safer for them if she was silenced too?

After all, if you'd murdered twice, what difference would a third make?

Chapter 22

A group of ponies and riders trotted out of the lane leading from the riding stables. Amber walked alongside them, so they hid her from view. Their hooves clattered on the cobblestones: her heart pounded almost as loudly.

She wasn't sure why she'd gone back to Hazelfield Lodge, the Blythes' house. Except it seemed the next logical step if she was to prove they were killers...

Before they killed her!

Somehow she had to make the police realize that murder had been committed. Only how could she, when there was no sign of any bodies? If only she had some proof of that couple's existence. The Blythes had destroyed everything. Photographs, documents, clothes – the lot.

If only she'd hung on to that photo. No one even believed there'd been a murder.

Not even Dean.

Reaching Hazelfield Lodge, Amber ducked out of view behind a rhododendron bush as the ponies trotted on. She remained, crouched among the foliage, peering between the huge pink flowers, breathing their sweet fragrance. Feeling like a spy.

Somehow, she had to take a closer look at that bonfire. If she could just salvage something from the ashes. Anything that would make Uncle Dave and the police investigate what had really happened to that old couple.

She stared at the long gravel driveway, trying to figure out some way of getting past Mr and Mrs Blythe.

Suddenly, the problem was solved for her!

The entire Blythe family came out of their house.

Amber held her breath as they got into their car.

"Yes," she whispered. "Go out! Go on, clear off. Just for half an hour … please … please…"

Jeremy Blythe started the engine and the car crawled slowly down the drive and out into the street.

Amber kept her head down as they headed towards town. The second they were out of sight, she dashed across the road, raced up their drive and hid amongst the shadows at the side of the building. Double-checking that no one was about, she ran down the garden to the remains of the bonfire.

The black heap of ashes hadn't been raked up. It lay there, the smell of burnt plastic lingering on the warm air.

Breathlessly Amber raked through the embers. Searching, scratching in the charred mass of rubble. But only the metal spines of the photograph albums remained. There were no photographs left – not one.

It was nothing but a black charred mess.

One or two scraps of unburnt paper remained at the perimeter of the fire however. She examined one. It had been a letter, the name Eastern Premium Oils was still legible and an address in a Far Eastern country. But the contents of the letter had been destroyed by flames.

Amber rubbed the charred bits away, leaving just a narrow scrap of paper with a company's name on. She pushed it into the back pocket of her shorts.

It wasn't much to go on. But there was nothing else.

Disappointed, she walked back up the garden and around the side of the house.

At the very same moment the Blythes decided to return.

Amber's blood froze.

Chapter 23

"What are you after?" Jeremy Blythe raged, leaping out of his car and striding towards her with a look of murder in his eyes.

Amber backed off, thinking fast. "I ... I was looking for Mrs Blythe. My aunt asked me to stop by and thank her for the jumble."

She looked Fiona Blythe in the eye and tried to smile. "My aunt says thanks so much, Mrs Blythe."

But her heart was racing. She could practically feel the incriminating piece of paper crawling out of her pocket.

And then to her horror, she became aware of her blackened hands and shoes. Her throat dried with fear. If they realized she was on to them…

Fiona Blythe stood shoulder-to-shoulder with her husband. "That's quite all right. If we come across any more jumble, we'll let you know."

Amber tried to smile, to look relaxed. But Jeremy Blythe's next comment almost made her choke.

"My daughter tells me you discovered a dead body in that old house on the cliffs yesterday."

"What? Oh no … er, not really…" Amber stuttered, trying to laugh it off. But her face twitched and her smile felt false. "It seems I was hallucinating, too much sun."

"So there wasn't any dead body?"

"No … no, not a thing."

"You got the police out though, to check," he went on, eyeing her accusingly.

"Yes, how did you know?"

Fiona Blythe answered for him. "We saw the police car and the officers heading that way." She smiled – coldly. "We see it all from here."

Amber broke out into a cold sweat. "Yes, well, it was nothing… Anyway, must get going. Thanks again for the jumble."

They moved aside and Amber edged past them. She'd done it, she was safe…

"Where on earth have you been to get your trainers that black!" Nina Blythe suddenly exclaimed.

The colour drained from Amber's cheeks. She glanced guiltily down at the ash on her shoes, but her mind was working swiftly. "The cliffs … I've been for a walk. It's that black slipper clay, it makes you filthy … it's all over my hands as well, see?"

She held out her hands. They all peered at them.

Clay or ash – would they know? Would they guess?

She held her breath – waiting.

With a dismissive toss of her head, Nina pushed past her. "You wouldn't catch me anywhere near those cliffs. They're dangerous."

Amber made her escape. She walked quickly, each step taking her away from the murderers. She only breathed again once she was out on the coastal road and heading towards town.

The library was easy to find.

It was cool and quiet inside. "I'm trying to find some information about an oil company," Amber told the librarian, showing her the piece of paper.

She didn't really expect her to be able to help, but, amazingly, the librarian unearthed a huge register-type book with a *Not For Loan* sticker on the spine. Amber watched silently, as the woman efficiently flicked through the pages.

Then to her astonishment, she pointed a slim finger at one of the entries – Eastern Premium Oils.

"Oh, thanks!" Amber exclaimed, reading the few words that merely gave the address, phone and fax numbers and a few other technical details. It gave no clue as to whether Jeremy and Fiona Blythe had murdered their parents.

Stupid of her to think it would.

"Any use?" asked the librarian.

"Not really. I'll make a note of the address…"

"What were you looking for exactly?"

She sighed. "I don't really know. Something about the people who worked there, I suppose."

"Wait a minute then," said the librarian and she went off to consult her computer. She returned a few minutes later. "There is one book that's been written on various oil companies in that area. It might be useful, only we don't stock it at this library. I could get it for you if you like."

"Yes, would you?"

The librarian filled out a green card. "Give me your telephone number and we'll contact you when it's in."

"Does it take long?"

She smiled. "I'll try and get it for tomorrow, but at the latest a week, so long as it's not out."

Thanking her, Amber went out of the cool peaceful atmosphere of the library and into the blazing sunshine. She was really nowhere nearer getting to the bottom of these murders.

She would have to think of something else.

*   *   *

Over dinner that evening, Dean eyed her curiously. "Where have you been all day? I've hardly seen you."

"Nowhere special. The library and just walking."

He pulled a face. "Wow! Exciting or what!"

Aunt Joan finished pouring the tea. "You should go to the library more often, Dean, it would keep you out of mischief."

"We're spending the day down in Slipper Bay tomorrow," Dean said, as he tucked into his meal. "You coming, Amber?"

"Who's we?" Amber asked, a sinking sensation in her stomach.

"Me and Nina."

The thought of spending a day with Nina filled her with dread. But worse was the thought of Nina alone with Dean. If she was as evil as Amber believed, then Dean could also be in danger.

"May as well," she murmured. She would have to warn Dean. Even if he didn't believe her. He had to be warned about what sort of person he was mixing with.

She would tell him tomorrow, on the way to the beach.

Thinking about the beach reminded her about the boat.

"Uncle Dave, there's a boat anchored in Slipper Bay. It belongs to the Blythes, doesn't it?"

"Blue one, The Mermaid?"

"Yes, that's the one."

"No, that's nothing to do with the new folk – that little boat belongs to Farmer Draper. It's his pride and joy!"

Amber stared at him. The sinister images in her head of the Blythes dragging the bodies down the cliff and into the boat suddenly fragmented to nothing.

Another image formed in her thoughts.

The shadow of a stocky farmer – looking down the barrel of a shotgun.

Chapter 24

"I've been doing a bit of digging today," Uncle Dave remarked, as he mopped up his gravy with a piece of bread.

Amber jumped. She had been lost in thought – thinking of Farmer Draper blasting someone with his gun, bundling them up in a carpet and dumping them out to sea. And the Blythes – had they been telling the truth all along? Was she being totally unfair to them?

"Not digging with a spade," Uncle Dave went on. "Just unearthing a few facts, something you asked me about the other day."

"Really?" she asked, suddenly interested in what he had to say.

"Mm, you asked if I knew anything about

the Blythes' parents. You said they were burning all their clothes and photos."

Her eyes widened. "What did you find out?"

"Only that Jeremy Blythe's parents died over twenty years ago. And as for Fiona Blythe, her folks passed away years before that."

Puzzled, Amber stared at him. "But that can't be…"

Uncle Dave continued. "That might explain why they were getting rid of their belongings. Who'd want to keep clothes that were twenty years old?"

"But that doesn't make sense!" Amber exclaimed. "They've just moved into Hazelfield Lodge – why would they bring their parents' old clothes with them."

"It doesn't really add up, Dad," Dean remarked. "Nina Blythe reckoned she quite liked her grandparents – do you remember her saying that, Amber?"

"Yes!" she said excitedly. "But she couldn't have known them if they died twenty years ago, she's only about our age."

"How old?" Aunt Joan murmured, a puzzled look on her face.

"And…" Dean went on, "there was that bundle of fivers in that suit pocket. They were new fivers, not ones they used years ago."

"Well, you've got me totally confused," Aunt Joan said, shaking her head. "It's perfectly obvious to me that Jeremy Blythe's been wearing that suit, whether it was his father's or not. I don't know what all the fuss is about. They're a perfectly respectable, nice couple."

"He couldn't have worn that suit, Aunty," exclaimed Amber. "It would have been too small."

Aunt Joan frowned. "I don't think so, Amber. It looked about right to me."

Amber said nothing. Her aunt's opinion of the *perfectly respectable* Blythes and her own opinion were vastly different.

Her aunt saw them as a lovely, generous old couple, while she saw them as a pair of mass murderers!

After dinner, Amber sat cross-legged at the bottom of Dean's bed. "I don't understand it, Dean. If Jeremy Blythe's parents actually died twenty years ago whose bodies were rolled up in the carpets?"

Dean groaned. "Amber ... I thought we'd decided. No bodies, no murderers ... you were hallucinating."

"No, I wasn't!" Amber declared fiercely.

He looked unconvinced. "Anyway, I thought you'd only seen one dead body, how come it's plural now?"

"There were *two* rolls of carpet..."

He burst out laughing. "Oh Amber, get real. People don't go around murdering other people and wrapping them up in carpets."

"I know what I saw!"

"You had sunstroke – you imagined it."

"It was nothing to do with the sun!" she shouted. "I saw a hand. It was dead and rotting ... you remember that awful smell in the house, don't you?"

He pulled a face. "Give it a rest, Amber, I've just had my dinner."

Angrily she gave him a shake. "Dean, will you listen, I'm deadly serious."

"Hey!"

"The Blythes have murdered two people,

burnt their clothes and every photograph of them. Put their bodies in a boat and dumped them out to sea. They've got away with double murder, Dean, and we've got to do something about it!"

"What boat, the one you just asked Dad about?"

"Yes, it had been moved…"

"Farmer Draper's boat?"

She heaved a confused sigh. "Yes, Farmer Draper's boat… I suppose the Blythes just took it."

Dean stared at her as if she were stupid. "It's a motor boat, Amber … don't you think it might need an ignition key?"

She blinked in confusion.

Dean spoke slowly and clearly. "The Blythes wouldn't have the key, because it's not their boat. So they couldn't have gone sailing with the dead bodies – could they?"

Her head began to swim. "They must have…"

"Think about it, Amber."

She fell silent, her thoughts tumbling about in her head. The scratch on her leg – if she had been hallucinating, then maybe she had scratched her leg on the barbed wire after all.

Maybe there were no dead bodies.

Perhaps she really was imagining everything.

Her head dropped, her hair trailed over her face. Dean lifted it and peered into her eyes. "Forget it, Amber. There are no dead bodies. The Blythes are a right funny lot I agree ... but they are *not* murderers. OK?"

Amber hardly slept a wink that night. She lay, tossing and turning, her thoughts a jumble in her brain.

When she finally slept, she dreamt of the Blythe family, walking along the beach, each dragging a dead body behind them.

Jeremy Blythe dragged an elderly man. His wife dragged the body of an old woman — there were frozen smiles on their faces, like in the photograph. Only now it looked hideous.

In her dream Amber wanted to run away. But first she had to see who Nina Blythe was dragging behind her.

Nina had hold of the dead person by the

ankles. Dragging the body over the sand. The body of a girl. Her hair was fair and long, it trailed behind, wiping over the tracks in the sand – so that no one would know.

Amber peered closer.

Sand covered the face of the dead person. Sand and maggots!

Sickened, Amber brushed them away with a black velvet cloth.

And then, with the sand and the maggots wiped away, a face stared up at her. Wide blue eyes. Dead sightless eyes.

Amber's eyes!

Amber's face!

The dead body was herself!

She awoke suddenly, with a jolt. Heart pounding. Cold sweat trickling down her back.

A dream … just a dream…

She breathed deeply, trying to slow the fierce drumming of her heart. Waiting for the panic and fear to subside.

It was a long time until she dared close her eyes again.

Chapter 25

"Telephone, Amber dear!" Aunt Joan called as Amber sat eating her breakfast.

"For me?" She hurried to the phone. "Hello?"

"Hayborough Library here," came the voice on the other end of the line. "Just letting you know that book you requested is in."

"That was quick! Thank you."

"We aim to please. If you'd like to call in over the next few days and pick it up."

"I'll come now."

Amber replaced the phone and went back to her breakfast. But she couldn't finish it. Her stomach had twisted itself into a knot.

"I thought you were coming to the beach with me and Nina?" Dean complained after she'd told him she was off to the library.

The mention of Nina Blythe's name brought the horror of the nightmare flooding back. She shuddered. The back of her neck started to prickle.

"I'll meet you down on the beach afterwards."

"Don't be long," Dean grumbled. "It might be the last chance you get."

Her stomach tightened. "What's that supposed to mean?"

"Means the weather's supposed to be changing. They're predicting storms."

"Oh, is that all..."

"Bad enough, isn't it? What's up with you anyway, you're all edgy and jumpy."

She headed for the door. "Nothing. Look, I'll be as quick as I can."

She fully intended being quick. The thought of Dean being alone with Nina Blythe was worrying. She was still positive that the Blythe family had committed murder. Maybe they hadn't used that little blue motor boat to dump the bodies – but there were other boats, weren't there?

If she was right – if this wasn't just her imagination – then Nina and her parents were very dangerous people.

She hurried into town and collected her book. A huge hefty tome that made her arms ache as she lugged it back across the clifftop path towards Slipper Bay.

Dean was probably right about the weather. It was still incredibly hot, but today it felt clammy, oppressive. The sky was a blanket of white cloud instead of its clear brilliant blue.

She shifted the book to under her other arm, beginning to doubt her sanity for ever requesting it. Even if she found something in it about Eastern Premium Oils, it was hardly likely to prove that the Blythes were cold-blooded murderers!

Reaching Slipper Bay, she clambered down the rockfall on to the beach. In the distance, she spotted two figures splashing about in the sea.

Dean and Nina.

Images of the nightmare rushed into her

head. She felt like turning and running. But Dean had spotted her. He waved his arms and she had no choice but to go down and join them.

"What on earth have you got there?" Nina exclaimed, eyeing the huge book under Amber's arm.

"This? It's…" She couldn't tell her. Couldn't risk Nina knowing that she was trying to get to the bottom of this mystery.

It was too dangerous.

"It's on medieval art," Amber lied. "Do you want to have a look?"

"No, thank you!" Nina said, turning up her nose. "Can't think of anything more boring."

"Hi there, Amber!" Dean called, wading out of the sea and heading towards her.

Nina looked from Amber to Dean, then ran straight at Dean. Laughing, she dragged him back into the sea.

Amber was glad they were out of the way. It gave her a chance to wade through the book for what she was looking for. First though, she spread out her towel and changed into her bathing costume. It was so hot!

The book made heavy reading, but there were plenty of photographs of oil refineries and oil rigs. And, to her delight, a long chapter on Eastern Premium Oils.

She had just found the right page when Dean came bounding up the beach, trailing water. Nina followed.

Amber quickly snapped the book shut.

Dean shook his head over her, showering her with sea spray.

"Dean! Watch it, this is a library book!"

"Boring!" mocked Nina, dabbing her face with her towel. "Oh, that sea is glorious. I don't know why you don't go for a swim, Amber, instead of sitting there reading a stupid book."

Amber's gaze swept over the waves, half expecting to see a corpse or two bobbing about on the waves. She shuddered. "I don't fancy it … you never know what gets dumped in the sea these days."

"That's true," Nina said agreeably, flopping down next to Dean a short way off.

Amber turned to the chapter on Eastern Premium Oils. She read quickly, her eyes swiftly scanning the photographs, always with one eye on Nina.

Nina and Dean sat skimming flat stones into the waves and talking. Amber paid little attention to their conversation.

"It's OK here, isn't it?" Nina was saying to Dean. "Where we used to live we were miles from the coast. And I love the sea. Surfing, snorkelling, sailing…"

Amber turned the page. There was a photograph…

"I'd like to go sailing," Dean was saying.

Amber stared hard at the photo. It was of a group of men in hard hats, standing beside a huge piece of oil refinery pipework. She peered closer. One of the faces looked familiar…

Nina and Dean were still talking…

"We *can* go sailing if you like, Dean."

"Hey, brilliant … do you fancy that, Amber? Hey Amber, wake up, I'm talking to you."

Amber stared at the photo. Read and reread the caption.

"Amber!"

"Oh, ignore her," muttered Nina. "Anyway, it's not sailing really, but at least it's a boat."

The photo had been taken seven years ago, according to the book. She reread the caption.

Eastern Premium Oil board of directors on a tour of the refinery on the occasion of director Jeremy Blythe's retirement – pictured centre of the group.

Amber's eyes widened.

Jeremy Blythe's retirement – but that wasn't Jeremy Blythe! That was the man in the little photograph. The man whose photographs and clothes had been destroyed.

Nina's grandfather – only that was imposs- ible because according to Uncle Dave he'd died twenty years ago.

A cool wind blew up suddenly, sending sand into her eyes – and a chill through her veins.

It could only mean one thing.

"I'll get the keys from my dad then," said Nina, jumping to her feet.

The Jeremy Blythe that they knew – Nina's

father – wasn't the real Jeremy Blythe at all! He was an impostor!

He must have murdered the real Jeremy Blythe and probably the real Fiona Blythe too – and taken over their identities – and wealth!

"That's not medieval art..." said Nina suddenly, accusingly, peering over Amber's shoulder.

Amber slammed the book shut, her heart hammering. Had Nina seen? Had she guessed that she knew the truth?

"What keys?" asked Dean.

For a second Nina didn't answer. Her face had paled. Then brightly she said, "That little motor boat moored out there."

"I thought that belonged to Farmer Draper," said Dean.

"Not any more," replied Nina. "We bought it off him last week."

Amber shivered violently – as the last piece of the jigsaw fell into place.

Chapter 26

"I'll nip home and borrow my dad's keys then," Nina repeated. Her face was pinched, her eyes as narrow and hard as her father's – whoever he was.

"Great!" said Dean, blissfully unaware of what was going on around him.

Amber remained silent, too stunned by what she'd just discovered to try and talk. She had to tell Dean. Just as soon as Nina left them alone.

"I won't be long," Nina said, clambering over some small rocks.

Go ... just go! Amber silently screamed.

You're an impostor!

You're a murderer!

Nina was almost out of earshot. Another few steps and she wouldn't be able to hear Amber telling Dean. He would have to believe her now – so would the police. The book was the proof she needed.

And no wonder Aunt Joan had a completely different impression of Mr and Mrs Blythe. She must have spoken to the real Blythes – just before they were murdered!

Suddenly Nina let out a cry of pain as she tumbled over the rocks and lay in a twisted heap – half in, half out of a rock pool.

Dean jumped to his feet and ran to her. "Nina … you OK?"

"Dean…!" Amber shouted after him.

But he was too intent on helping Nina. He lifted her out of the pool. She was soaked and dazed.

Overhead, the sun crawled behind a black cloud and hid.

"Nina … are you all right?"

She opened one eye. "Oh my head … my ankle…"

"These rocks are dead slippery," fretted Dean.

Nina tried to stand, but her ankle gave way and she cried out in pain. "It's twisted... Oh! It really hurts."

Amber stooped down to examine it. "It hasn't swollen, it's probably nothing serious."

"And you'd know, would you?" Nina snapped. Then in a softer voice, she said to Dean, "I'll never make it back home on my own now... Will you help me?"

"Course, we both will."

"No, Amber can stay here and keep an eye on all our things. It'll save packing everything up."

"Makes sense," Dean nodded. "We won't be long, Amber."

Amber glanced up at the darkening sky. "I think there's a storm coming... I may as well come with you."

"It's just a cloud," Dean dismissed, putting an arm around Nina's waist. "It'll pass."

Amber took a step back. She didn't really want to go to the Blythes' house anyway – especially now. She would get the chance to speak to Dean later.

Besides, she wanted to take a look on board

that boat before Nina got to it. Possibly there'd be a clue, fragments of carpet. Something ... anything.

She watched them go, Nina hobbling and Dean holding her up. It took them ages to reach the top. And meanwhile more and more grey clouds rolled in.

As soon as they'd disappeared from view, Amber made her move. She ran along the beach, getting as close as possible to where the boat was moored.

Then waded out.

The sea felt colder than usual, and choppier. White-capped waves rolled up and washed over her. She bobbed and jumped them, diving over some, through others, until she was up to her neck. And then she swam the last few metres to the little blue boat.

Hauling herself on board was the hardest thing. But once on, she scoured it for clues.

The boat rocked and bobbed. The wind was getting up. This wasn't a good day for going out on a boat...

The floor was wet, a small puddle had gathered at one end. Suddenly the boat dipped and the puddle ran to the opposite end of the boat. Amber's stomach churned over.

White-crested waves were gathering. The wind whipped her hair over her eyes and the boat flipped sideways. The next wave broke over the side of the boat and flooded it.

There were no clues to the murder – stupid of her to think there would be.

She sat on the wooden slatted seat, ankle-deep in sea water, clinging to the sides of the rolling, rocking boat, and heard the first rumble of thunder in the distance.

A storm *was* coming.

She had to get back to shore – and quickly.

She lowered herself into the sea, gasping as a wave broke over her head and, for a few moments, she floundered about under water, spluttering.

Catching hold of the side of the boat again, she clung to it while she got her breath. But the waves were growing fierce, battering her against the boat's hull.

Another rumble of thunder – louder, and a sudden violent flash of lightning across the horizon.

She *had* to get to shore!

Bracing herself, she took a deep breath, and waited for a lull in the waves. Then launching herself away from the boat, she swam as hard as she could.

Despite it being just a few metres before she was back in her depth, it was difficult going. The tide was still going out. She could feel the fierce pull of the current, making every stroke ten times more difficult.

She forced herself on. Arms and lungs crying out in pain as she swam against the tide.

At last. Her toes felt the soft sand of the sea bed. She struggled on, half swimming, half wading on to the shore.

On dry land, she sank to her knees, gasping for breath.

That had been a stupid idea – and dangerous!

She was cold now. The sun was blanketed in thick black, ominous clouds. A fierce gusting wind whipped the sand up into her face, half blinding her.

She staggered back along the beach,

fighting against the wind to where she had left all her belongings. Her book had been blown open and the pages fluttered wildly in the wind. Towels and clothing were being blown all over the beach.

She ran around like a mad thing. Gathering everything up. Struggling to see, with her hair and the sand in her eyes. Struggling to breathe as the wind blasted in, snatching her breath away.

The first drops of rain splashed down on her head as she began to climb the rockfall to the cliff path.

Big, cold raindrops that pierced her T-shirt and chilled her skin instantly.

Another flash of lightning crackled over the horizon. More thunder – low and rumbling – threatening.

And a fierce gust of wind that almost took her feet from beneath her.

She clung on to the mossy boulders, alarmed as some of the smaller stones suddenly began to jump and roll downwards, like a tiny avalanche.

Darkness fell. A horrible unnatural

blackness like twilight, despite it being only morning.

She shivered. Everything seemed unreal. Nightmarish.

There was no one on the cliff path. It lay windswept and deserted. She turned her feet towards the town, just as the wind brought the rain lashing in from the ocean in a grey misty wet cloud.

Through the mist, Amber glimpsed a figure coming towards her.

Her heart almost stopped.

A ghostly, misty figure…

As it neared, Amber saw that it was no ghost. Even so, her stomach tightened.

Nina!

"You're here!" Nina gasped. She was soaked to the skin and her hair clung to her pale thin face. "Why did you go to the old house? Where's Dean?"

"What are you talking about?" cried Amber, shouting to be heard over the howling of the wind.

"When the storm broke, we started back for you… We bumped into the chap from the farm. He said you'd gone to the old house. Dean was frantic – he took off to bring you back."

"That's crazy ... why would he say that?" Her heart thumped, thoughts racing. Was Farmer Draper involved in this after all? Was this some sort of trick to get Dean alone at the house?

Her thoughts pounded in her brain.

"I begged him not to go!" Nina cried. She looked distraught. She could barely stand with the pain in her ankle. "We've got to do something... I'll go and fetch my dad..."

That would take for ever, Amber thought; Nina could hardly walk, let alone run.

"No ... go and ring for Dean's dad," Amber instructed. "He'll be at the police station... I'm going after Dean."

"Right ... I'll be as quick as I can," Nina promised, and hobbled away through the rain.

Amber began to run. But the weight of all the wet bags slowed her down. There was nothing else for it – she bundled them all under a bush and hoped everything would still be there when she got back.

A dreadful black sensation swept over her.
As if something terrible was about to happen.
A thought jumped into her head.
Would she be back?
Ever?

Chapter 27

Drenched to the skin, her legs crying out in agony, Amber forced herself on towards Lord Devlin's old house.

The rain lashed in from the sea. The wind roared and howled and gusted, blowing her off track. And it was all she could do to make sure she didn't stray too close to the edge of the cliff as she ran.

Cutting across Farmer Draper's land, she hesitated, afraid in case he was watching. Hiding in the bushes, near to where the cows had gathered, huddled together for comfort, as the storm broke.

Why had the farmer told Dean she'd come this way? It was a lie. A trick. Perhaps Farmer Draper was the guilty one after all.

Why else would he have lied to Nina?

She felt sick.

What if he was murdering Dean right this second ... rolling his body into a carpet ... leaving it to rot...

She stumbled on, running as fast as she could. Until at last, exhausted, she came to the old house.

The ground was muddy here, a black slippery mud. The cracks in the earth had filled with rainwater and her feet slid and slithered as she picked her way around to the gap in the barbed wire.

"Dean ... Dean ... it's me ... Amber ... I'm out here!"

The wind swept her cries away. A crackle of lightning lit up the sky, followed almost instantly by an explosion of deafening thunder.

She covered her ears, cringed against the force of the storm.

"Dean..." The ground seemed to shift. A puddle of dirty water oozed up from a widening crack and covered her feet. She jumped back, slipping on the black mud. "Dean! Get out of the house!"

Frantic, Amber scrambled and slithered back up the slope, peering back across the rain-swept clifftops. Nina must have phoned for help by now.

The police would race here.

Wouldn't they?

She slipped on the wet grass and landed on her knees. Scrambling to her feet, she saw something approaching. A vague form coming towards her through the blanket of mist and rain.

Her hopes rose – and fell in one heart-stopping second.

She stood, trembling.

Her eyes so wide with fear that the rain half blinded her. Her breathing quickened. She felt the awful sensation of panic ... of terror.

A bolt of jagged forked lightning zigzagged overhead, illuminating the black sky in a flash of electric blue.

Illuminating the figure thundering towards her through the gloom...

The phantom Lord Devlin astride his ghostly white horse!

He got within metres of Amber. She felt the vibrations, heard the thudding of hooves...

And then he stopped.

Horse and rider remained perfectly still. Unafraid of the storm, and the blinding, flashing lightning and the explosions of thunder.

The phantom sat high upon his mount – staring down at her.

Staring through those black hollow eye sockets of his skull head.

Amber screamed.

A scream of stark terror.

But her cry was swallowed up by the noise of the storm.

No one heard her.

Except the phantom.

Chapter 28

Her heart was thumping.

Slowly, terrified, Amber walked – tried to walk – around the awful apparition. Giving it a wide berth. Her eyes riveted to it.

She saw him move. Just one tiny movement of his heel against the horse's side, and the animal obeyed.

They turned, remaining eye-to-eye with Amber.

She could hardly breathe.

She trod warily, slowly, afraid to make any sudden movement. But each step she took, the horse moved with her. Backing up, so she couldn't get beyond it.

"What do you want?" Amber uttered.

In response the phantom Lord Devlin reared his horse up on its hind legs and brought it around, barring her way completely.

She jumped back, her eyes wide with fear.

Steam rose from the horse's body. An eerie white mist mingling with the cloud and rain. Lord Devlin's black velvet cloak billowed out in the wind. Flapping like a giant bat's wing.

His black fathomless eyes continued to stare.

"Let me pass..." she whispered, trying again to go around him. But a flick of his booted heel and the horse responded, snorting, growing agitated.

"Please! Get out of my way!"

She started to run. But the horse and rider were swifter, more agile on this boggy ground.

She stopped.

Ran the other way.

Dodged.

Turned.

But whatever she tried, they were quicker, effectively halting every attempt at escape.

"What do you want?" she screamed, terror mingling with anger now.

The rain lashed down, her hair clung like

rats' tails to her face. And the phantom Lord Devlin urged his horse forward.

Towards her!

"No … go away!"

Forward they came, phantom and horse.

Step by step. Inch by inch. Closer and closer.

Amber stumbled backwards. Back towards the house.

"No! I'm not going in there – it's not safe!" she screamed through the howling wind. And she made a dash for freedom.

But again he was too quick. Like lightning he cut off her escape.

And then again, slowly, menacingly, he inched his horse towards her, the animal taking short, neat, purposeful steps towards her.

"Oh no!" Amber breathed, glancing behind her. "No … you can't!"

Terror screamed through her. No longer was he forcing her back towards the old house…

He was forcing her over the cliff!

She felt the full force of the wind blast into her. Sensed the dangerous drop down to the rocks far, far below. Felt the ground shift and slide beneath her feet.

"No!" she screamed. "You can't ... I won't let you... You're dead ... you're nothing but a ghost!" And she ran full pelt at rider and horse, convinced she would be able to run straight through the apparition.

Ghost weren't real. They were images.

The bulk of the horse and a kick from the rider's boot sent Amber tumbling backwards into the mud.

For a second she couldn't speak ... couldn't think straight. Then realized that whatever this vision was, it was as solid and real as she was – only much, much stronger.

"What are you...?" she breathed, as the horse and rider regained their stance.

She backed away again ... towards the house. "What do you want from me?"

She felt the hollow of the land beside the old house. Felt the jagged barbed wire pricking into her skin.

She had no choice.

It was the house, or the cliff.

And either meant death!

Chapter 29

Amber scrambled between the barbed wire, catching her T-shirt and hair on the barbs. Barely noticing.

Once through, she dragged the two cut edges of the wire closer and tried to twist them together.

She felt a small glimmer of hope as she realized the hole was too small for the phantom and horse to get through. For a second, she stood there, looking at them through the barbed wire. For the moment, safe.

But to her horror, he simply dismounted. Expertly swinging down from the horse. Amber glimpsed a flash of silver as he drew a long glinting sword from his belt and strode towards her.

With a scream, she dived into the house and slammed the door shut.

The house shuddered and shook with the force of the door being banged into place. She pressed herself up against the timber, trying to calm the old house. Trying to stop the shaking.

And then she realized it was *her* who was shaking. Trembling from head to toe.

Shaking with fear.

There was a bolt on this side of the door. Desperately Amber tried to push it into place. But it was too rusted and refused to budge.

Panic rising, she ran through the house, calling out Dean's name... Where was he?

Up the stairs, feeling them sway, hearing the groans and creaks of the timber. The whole house seemed to be moving, swaying, groaning. As if it were speaking to her.

Lamenting its fate – and hers.

There seemed no escape – for either of them.

Upstairs, Amber raced through every

room, throwing the doors wide, searching for Dean. Each time, bracing herself to finding him lying dead.

The final room – at the end of the corridor. The room where the bodies had been stored, wrapped in carpet.

She hesitated. Afraid to go in. Slowly she turned the handle – slowly she pushed open the squeaking door.

The room was empty.

No rolled-up carpets. No dead bodies. No Dean.

Outside the wind blasted against the boarded-up windows. Rattling the wood. Wailing through the cracks. While the rain beat down and the thunder boomed.

Then she heard it. Another sound…

Footsteps on the stairs.

Slow, heavy footsteps.

Clinking metal buckles against black leather boots.

Thud-thudding. Up the stairs – towards her.

Terror froze her to the spot.

The phantom…

Chapter 30

He stood in the doorway – Lord Devlin – the phantom. Sword in his gloved hand. Black velvet cloak dripping with rain. Rain dripping from the cowl that half shrouded his stark white parched bone face.

Black soulless eyes stared at her.

Amber's legs buckled. She felt faint. A black, hot swampy feeling flooded over her and she pressed herself against the wall for support.

"What … what do you want?" she uttered. The words would barely come. Her throat was thick with fear.

It spoke. A whispering, distant sound. "I want you out of the way… You're not going to spoil things for us now ... not after all the trouble we've gone to."

"I don't understand."

"Then allow me to explain."

That voice! She recognized it!

Very slowly, the phantom took hold of his own white bony chin. Amber watched, mesmerized, as slowly a rubber-skull mask was peeled away, revealing the true identity of the phantom.

Jeremy Blythe! Or the man pretending to be Jeremy Blythe.

"You!" she breathed.

He smiled. A cold sinister smile. But his eyes remained as stark and cold as when they were behind the mask.

"What do you think of my little disguise? A perfect way of keeping nosy people like yourself away from the old house till the tides were right to dispose of the bodies." His face twisted into a sneer. "Nice outfit, don't you think? I *borrowed* it from the local museum – when they weren't looking."

"You killed the real Mr and Mrs Blythe, didn't you...?" Amber uttered, her fear dissolving, turning into something else…

"Clever girl, you worked it out. Nina said you had, when she saw you looking at that book with the photo of old Jeremy in it. Must admit, that was something I overlooked … and the fact that your aunt got to meet them before we, er, disposed of them."

"You won't get away with this. My uncle will be on his way here now…"

"Why will he?" he said coldly. "You don't really think Nina has rung him do you? And you didn't really believe Dean was here, and all that about the farmer!" He threw back his thin head and laughed.

Amber felt her anger rise.

"Oh and don't worry yourself about Nina's ankle – that was a little fib too."

"Why?" Amber breathed, her voice just a whisper, barely audible over the crashing of the storm outside.

"My wife and I worked for the real Jeremy and Fiona Blythe after they'd retired," he said coolly, threading the skull mask over the sharp tip of his sword, running the blade through the eye socket as he spoke. "I was his chauffeur, my wife did their cleaning... The Blythes were *so* wealthy."

"So you killed them," Amber whispered, sickened. "And took their identities."

His thin mouth curled. "That's right. And everything was going so well until you started snooping around."

"Where's Dean?" she demanded, her voice rising.

"Home I imagine. My daughter puts on a good act when she has to. A lie about a twisted ankle fooled you both. Another lie when she came home sent him scuttling off – forgot all about you."

"What lie?" Amber breathed. "What did she say?"

"My lie actually – mine and my wife's," he admitted, smiling coldly. "Luckily Nina managed to tell us quickly what had happened, so we came up with the story that his mother had phoned – frantic she was – something about his dad being involved in an accident. He shot off – leaving Nina to go back to you and send you in this direction. Clever don't you think?"

"So what happens to me now?"

Slowly he withdrew the sword from the eye socket of the mask. Evil sparked from his eyes. "This delightful sword was another *gift* from our local museum by the way … and as to your question, I'm afraid you've left me with no choice…"

Lightning flashed above the house. An enormous explosion of electricity lit up the room. A terrific crash of thunder followed, and the house shook.

Anger rose up inside Amber. A fury she couldn't halt. And with every ounce of strength she possessed, she charged at him, catching him off-balance. The sword clattered to the floor, and Amber raced past him, along the balcony and down the stairs.

But the stairs moved, swaying like some fairground ride. She gripped the banisters as she struggled down.

Then came a violent lurch and the entire house seemed to rock on its foundations.

Cracks suddenly appeared in the walls – as if someone had drawn them in with a huge pen.

The chandelier swayed – back and forth, tinkling, chinking

The house timbers creaked and groaned and cried out as if in pain.

Amber froze as another almighty cracking sound filled the air and the marble floor split in two, as if an earthquake had struck.

He appeared at the top of the swaying, moving stairs. There was terror in his eyes. "What's happening? Help me!"

Everything seemed to be moving. The house swayed back and forth before her very eyes. Amber screamed, "The house is going over…"

But before he could move, the staircase gave one incredible crashing sound and broke free from the balcony. Collapsing on to the marble floor like a pack of cards. The balcony dipped at a frightening angle, and he ran back into a bedroom.

"Get out!" Amber shrieked.

The crack in the floor widened. Massive lumps of plaster dropped down from the ceiling. Shattering on the floor.

Above her, the chandelier began to tinkle

louder ... then a ripping, cracking sound. The ceiling gave way and the chandelier dropped.

Amber leapt aside as it splintered into a million sparkling fragments.

She raced to the door, heart thudding. The house was going over... He was trapped upstairs ... she had to get help.

She yanked at the back door. It refused to budge!

The door-frames had warped, lodging it tight. Frantically Amber pulled and pulled as behind her the house screamed out in agony.

And then suddenly it opened. Cold rain and wind blasted in. Outside thunder and lightning created havoc.

She ran out into the storm. Squeezed through the barbed wire, horrified at the sight of all the massive cracks that had appeared in the ground all around the house.

The cliff was crumbling ... taking the house with it.

She had to get help...

Through the rain she saw a car parked on the cliff. Mrs Blythe – or whoever she really was – and Nina were running from it, towards her.

"Where's my husband?" the woman shrieked.

"In the house… But…"

They pushed her out of the way. Scrambled through the hole in the barbed wire – and disappeared into Lord Devlin's house.

Frantic, Amber ran to where the car stood on higher ground. She could barely see, rain and tears were blinding her.

Then suddenly came the noise.

She swung round.

A dreadful groaning, splintering, dying sound was coming from the house, as it slowly, slowly collapsed.

The earth gave way. A whole massive chunk of ground broke away from the cliff – and the house began to slip.

The chimneys broke off first. Then slates, that skidded down the roof.

And then, quite suddenly, as if someone had opened a trapdoor, Lord Devlin's once magnificent house simply dropped out of sight.

Taking with it Nina and her parents.

The sound of it smashing on the rocks below made Amber fall to the ground and cover her ears. A huge cloud of dust billowed up and hovered in the air, almost in the shape of a ghostly house itself.

And then it settled.

A deathly silence fell.

So silent was the sound, that it hurt.

Chapter 31

The wailing of police sirens finally broke the eerie silence. Lightning was flashing out to sea now, the thunder a distant rumble.

Three police cars screeched along the cliff path. Finally skidding to a halt. Half a dozen policemen jumped out. Uncle Dave was there too – and Dean.

They all came to a dead stop at the sight that met their eyes – the gaping hole where the house had stood.

No one spoke.

Slowly, Amber walked towards her uncle and Dean.

She put her arm around Dean's shoulder. "I'm sorry, Dean, but Nina was in the house when it went over – and her parents."

Tears formed in his eyes. "Least it weren't you."

"They murdered the real Jeremy and Fiona Blythe," she quietly explained to her uncle. "And took their identities. They must have been planning it for ages. They used the legend of the phantom as a way of keeping people away from the old house until they'd got rid of the bodies. Aunty Joan nearly spoiled their plans, she was the only one to ever meet the real Blythes. No wonder she thought the Blythes were a lovely old couple!"

Uncle Dave took his jacket off and wrapped it around Amber's shoulders. "I'm sorry we didn't believe you, Amber."

She nodded.

Dean rubbed his sleeve across his eyes. "Nina tricked us all. Tricked me into dashing home, so you'd be alone…"

Amber's gaze drifted over the gaping chasm. "Well, this was one trick that went horribly wrong."

Uncle Dave gave the order to his men to call the coastguard – and for Amber and Dean to get into the car.

There was nothing anyone could do here.

"Hey, sir!" one of the officers shouted.

Everyone looked.

A policeman emerged from the bushes, leading a beautiful white horse.

The phantom's horse.

No longer afraid, Amber went over and stroked its wet face. It nuzzled against her.

"It's one of the horses from the stables just up the road," Uncle Dave remarked. "I'll get someone to take it back. But in the meantime, let's get you two home and dry."

They were driven back through the clinging grey mist that lingered over the cliff tops. Amber wiped the windows and peered back at the spot where the house had stood.

But something else caught her eye. She squinted, rubbed her eyes, rubbed the window again.

It was still there, out on the cliff top...

She grabbed Dean's arm and silently pointed...

They both peered out, through the window, through the drizzle.

"Dean ... do you see them?" Amber whispered.

"I see – I just don't believe!"

She rolled down the window. Two hazy, white images seemed to hover just above the ground. Two people on horseback. Dressed in old-fashioned clothes.

Amber remembered that very first morning when she thought she'd seen two riders through the heat haze.

Lord Devlin – the *real* Lord Devlin and his wife, Isabella. She had glimpsed the real phantoms then – and now.

But they weren't ugly or terrifying – they looked beautiful and at peace. They were holding hands and smiling at each other.

As she and Dean watched, they slowly faded away.

Amber sighed. "Someone had better rewrite that book on legends. There's not one phantom rider haunting these cliffs – there's two!"

"Doesn't it scare you?" Dean asked.

She smiled and shook her head. "No, at least we know Lord Devlin isn't still roaming these cliff tops searching for his wife, like the legend says. They're together – for all eternity. I think that's so romantic."

Dean gave a little shudder. "Pretty spooky though, don't you reckon? *Real* ghosts! Aren't you just a little bit scared?"

"Course not," Amber told him truthfully. Then added a little warily, "Well, they don't scare me at the moment. But don't you dare suggest we go out in the middle of the night to investigate!"

"Ah, come on Amber – where's your sense of adventure?"

She gasped and he laughed.

"I'm joking – honest."

Amber cast him a warning glance. "You'd better be joking, Dean Brewster ... you'd better be!"